"This picture is taken a hundred years from now. The disaster it records, on the face of it, is going to happen within the next few months. And it isn't local. Just look at the mountain chain outside the cave. . . ."

The time: now.

The speaker: the chief of a top secret U.S. time probe project.

The place: a guarded cavern in Tennessee.

The discovery: utter planetary catastrophe on its way.

The volunteer: a man to go forward into the future to determine

(a) what caused the end of the world,

(b) what could be done to prevent it.

The price: his life, his girl's life, his country's life, his world's life.

REX GORDON writes: "My readers do not write to compliment me on the way I have used some fancy and unlikely scientific theory to produce a trick ending. What they want to know is, will it really be like that; is that true; is that what modern scientific thinking may mean to us? They want to know which way life is going, and so do I. They want to know what aspects of life are permanent and what are likely to turn out to be merely the current superstitions and social mores of our place and time.

"I have to be on my toes to keep up with them and to produce books which are fit and worthy for them to read. But it is an exciting and demanding game, and when I think how H. G. Wells' sociological fantasies have affected the modern world, and how the Utopias of the past from Plato to Samuel Butler have affected modern thinking, I do not think it is a useless one. Frankly, I think the critics are stupid when they fail to see in science-fiction some of the most important writing of our time. For science-fiction belongs to that class of literature that is read by people who are tolerant, who know how little we know, but who have guts and who think."

FIRST THROUGH TIME

REX GORDON

ACE BOOKS, INC.
1120 Avenue of the Americas
New York 36, N.Y.

Ace Books by Rex Gordon include:

FIRST ON MARS (D-233)
FIRST TO THE STARS (D-405)

I

WE WERE COMING out from the rock tunnels of the synchrotron, out into the morning sunlight and the view across Lake Valley from below the cliff face.

A man came across from the apron where we had parked the cars. He walked between Sara and Strassen and put his hand upon my shoulder.

He said, "Conference, Judge."

"What conference?" I said.

"Galbraith will be at the conference," he said, "and so will all the important people." He took me to his car.

He was the man who had welcomed me, stepping out from nowhere, when I had arrived at the university the previous night. Maybe it was because he had not had time then, that he had not explained who he was and why.

The 'important people' apparently did not include Strassen or Sara Francis. They were left behind when he closed his car door, started it, and drove towards the road that wound up the valley side to the university.

"Curiosity is frowned on in this part of the country," I said. "And people don't ask questions."

"What do you want to know?" he said.

"Your name," I said. "Or, failing that, if I'm to take orders from you, your rank and status."

"Carl Reckman," he said. "Military intelligence."

He put the car into the bends on the winding road.

"What has military intelligence to do with this?" I said.

"This work is being done under an appropriation for military intelligence now," he said. "It has to be done under some appropriation. You ask the Senator."

"What Senator?"

He said, "You'll meet him."

There was a helicopter parked on the grass between the buildings of the university. There were also two large cars with uniformed drivers. I wondered if the government was moving in.

Out of the car, Reckman led me up a flight of marble steps. "They're holding it in the projection room," he said. "There's that about a university. It has the places."

A man at the door looked closely even at Reckman before he let us in. Inside, the lights were on in a room with a projector and a screen. I saw Galbraith's great gray head even before I saw his hunched and shambling untidy figure. There were three other men, one in General's uniform.

It is hard to describe the impression Galbraith had made on me. We had had scientists, engineers and technicians of all descriptions at the rocket base, and I had thought he would be one of them. He wasn't. It was not a difference in quality. He was a different kind of man. In some ways he was more homely and less restrained. At other times, while he went on using the simplicities of ordinary speech, you found he was losing you in the most complicated matters which he all too obviously expected you to easily understand.

"Here are Reckman and Major Judgen now," he said. He looked at his projectionist who was fixing a film in his machine. "Shall we put the lights out? We may as well begin."

There was a slight delay while the introductions were performed.

"Major, this is Secretary Stephens," Reckman said. "The Major is our volunteer, Mr. Secretary. If anyone does this thing, he will. Senator, this is Major Howard Judgen . . ."

I was saluting. I had recognized General Bridger. It was

not from previous personal acquaintance. I had seen his picture. Who hasn't? The sight and fact of him there gave me a new idea of the importance of whatever it was we were trying to do. It put it in a new class.

"Are you a volunteer, Major?" the General asked me.

"I don't know yet, sir," I told him. "I don't know what I am volunteering for."

He grinned, making all those assumptions that Generals are inclined to make.

Secretary Stephens was making an objection to Galbraith, who, to move us to the chairs, was having his projectionist put the lights out one by one.

"I don't see why you want us to see this film, Professor. Film reports and scientific records of experiments are surely a matter of evaluation by the experts."

"Experts aren't deciding whether we send a man instead of cameras next time, Mr. Stephens," Galbraith said. For a moment he looked past the Secretary at me, and then at the General beside me. It was obvious whom he thought would do the deciding. I wondered why the Secretary and the Senator were there at all. As Reckman had said, I soon found out. We were moving to the chairs. Galbraith's personality or whatever it was worked. He was treating us as a captive audience.

The Senator and the Secretary were fretting. At their level of government they must have thought it a departure from custom to begin a conference with an attempt to learn facts directly. "How am I to tell the appropriations committee?" the Senator said. "I can't just tell them that it's a matter of bookkeeping, the transfer to Intelligence of an item of equipment costing a hundred million dollars."

"You can tell them it's secret," Galbraith said. "We're very secret here. If there are questions, tell them the truth, that even we don't know quite what we're doing." And he nodded to his projectionist who put the final light out. He said: "Why should we be able to explain it?"

We sat in the dark looking towards the blank screen, not

like a conference so much as a university class that had come to hear a lecture. Then the screen came to life.

I recognized the picture. I had just come from there. It was the big underground laboratory at the target end of the synchrotron. But Galbraith had to tell the others.

"This is where we actuate the controls and work when the synchrotron is in operation," he said. "You can see that we, the operating staff, are all on one side of a barrier wall. Everything that happens around the target is dealt with by that robot machinery you can see on the other side. Even this camera that took these pictures could have been shielded had we thought it necessary."

The screen showed us a picture of the human operating side of the laboratory as we watched it in the darkened room. Galbraith himself could be seen in the picture, controlling and observing the experiment. William Strassen was standing near the barrier wall. Sara Francis was sitting at the control desk watching the many dials and switches of the synchrotron itself.

The camera showed her hand hovering over the many dials and switches and then swung up and showed us a clock on the wall over her head reading three minutes to noon.

"This is an actual experiment," Galbraith said. "Our most recent and most rewarding, if you can call it that. It is what made me call you here. That girl is Sara Francis, a young assistant. We use her because she has perfectly mastered the art of setting up the situation in which these events happen. I am not telling you this for human interest. She features later in the film."

The camera evidently swung again, for the picture of the laboratory swung and we found ourselves looking across the barrier wall. The screen showed us the target area of the synchrotron. But the "target", if it could be called that, at the point the beam would strike, was another camera and a group of instruments, on a plinth, under an inverted glass bowl or bell-jar.

The other camera was trained back on the laboratory so

that while the one that had taken the film we were seeing saw it, it would in turn look back at our camera, at the clock on the laboratory wall, and at Sara, Strassen and Galbraith.

"Two cameras watching one another," Galbraith said. "And what is more, two clocks."

The screen showed us a close-up of the camera and instruments inside the bell-jar and one of them was a clock, the time on which corresponded with that of the clock on the wall of the laboratory.

The other instruments were a thermometer, a barometer, and a radiation meter, all of the recording type.

"The aim is to put a man in the place of those instruments," Galbraith said.

In the semi-darkness of the projection room, visible only from the light reflected by the screen, everyone was watching intently. The screen now showed us a general view of Sara adjusting her controls and closing switches and of the laboratory clock at noon, and then once again it showed us the bell-jar in the target area on the other side of the wall with the second camera and the instruments inside it.

At first nothing seemed to happen. Bell-jar and instruments looked lifeless as the power of the synchrotron was directed on them. Then the hands of one of them came to life and began to move. It was the clock.

Only a few seconds had passed, and yet the small clock among the instruments was registering three minutes past the hour. The movement of the hands became visible after that. They moved round the clock face with increasing speed. I looked at the other instruments. The radiation meter was up a bit, but not to an extent to endanger human life.

"What is this?" Secretary Stephens said. "Have you speeded up the film?"

The camera answered him. The screen's view of the laboratory tilted and swung and we saw Sara again, watching her control desk carefully, and the wall clock behind her. The wall clock said two minutes after twelve, but when the view returned to the target again, the clock among the instruments in the bell-jar was reading one o'clock and the hands were speeding on.

Something else was happening too. It was as though a mist, a cloud, was forming in quite a large area around the bell-jar. It made any observation of the clock, the second camera, and the other instruments inside the bell-jar difficult. The clock among the instruments could just be seen to be reading something to three and then it was obscured by a darkening fog.

What we were seeing now was a misty sphere, perhaps five feet in diameter, that totally enclosed the bell-jar. And the sphere darkened. It became opaque. Gradually, it became wholly black, as though we were seeing a hole in space.

Thinking of what Galbraith had said about putting a man in the place of those instruments, camera and clock that had disappeared, I could not say I liked it. I did not see why they should do it, either.

"That is what happens," said Galbraith. "The instruments go. We keep the experiment in operation for half an hour, and then release, and they come back. Now I propose to show you the same thing, and further, as it is recorded on the second camera's film."

He gave orders to the projectionist to stop the film he was showing, which was showing a static scene in the laboratory, and transfer to the film that had been taken from the second camera on its return.

"You have a volunteer who will go and sit there, in the target area of your synchrotron, and let that sphere form round him?" the Senator said. "In what are you trying to involve the government? In licensed suicide?"

"If the recording instruments say a man can survive, then he can survive," the General said. "Major Judgen and his kind have been into all that in their experiments for outer space."

It was dark and then light and then dark again in the projection room as the operator switched spools in his projector, and then we were watching film again.

This time it was the film taken by the camera inside the bell-jar.

10

It looked the same to begin with. There was Galbraith and Strassen, with Sara at the control desk, and the clock above her head that said noon, all taken from the point of view I would have if I were sitting out there in the "hot" side of the laboratory and looking back at them through the mirrors above the barrier wall.

But this camera did not shift around as the other had. We had to watch for ourselves. We could see Sara making the final movements on her board in response to a word from Galbraith, and then it was the laboratory wall clock above her that speeded up.

I looked at it and looked again. Its hands too were going round the dial with increasing speed. And then I saw something odd in Strassen's movements as he appeared on the screen. He was adjusting some of the robot handling machinery they kept in position around the target area, and he had to go from one part of the laboratory to another. He moved jerkily and with increasing, and then with fantastic speed.

Secretary Stephens said: "Wait! There's something wrong! If it were true that time in that fishbowl from which this film was taken was speeded up, then this clock should be shown going slower, not faster!"

"You see why I wanted you to see for yourself," said Galbraith.

"He's right!" said the Senator. "Here you've got two clocks speeding up, each when seen from the other's viewpoint. It casts doubt on your whole experiment!"

"I'd agree if we knew anything about time," Galbraith said. "It seems we don't."

"Before this, no one's succeeded in affecting it in any way," said Bridger.

Even Reckman spoke up diffidently. "We had our experts puzzle about this," he said. "They talked of different and divergent time-tracks."

Galbraith made no comment. I thought perhaps he did not want to get into an argument with the Intelligence experts. He had been simpler. He had just said he did not know the answer.

11

But arguments and questions were stopped by what was happening on the screen. In the other film we had seen a dark opaque sphere form around the camera out of which we were now looking. But the camera in the target did not record it that way. What was obscuring the view of the laboratory and of the clock, which said twenty to three by then, and of the view of the blurred, uncertain darting shapes of Sara, Galbraith and Strassen (we were getting pictures of them even after the experiment was over, Strassen told me later), was a luminous, pearly mist.

The screen suddenly showed us pictures of nothing but a wavering light, and then a total darkness.

"Over-exposed and then under-exposed," Galbraith said.

The screen had become light again.

"This is where the inexplicable part begins," said Galbraith.

The screen was showing us alternate light and darkness in a rapid succession that was slowing down like a television picture warming. And there was something in those pictures if only, straining our eyes in the projection room, we could see them.

Then the picture steadied. The alterations of light and dark became slower until, with a last heave, the picture held.

I heard an audible gasp in the projection room. It was only as I heard it that I realized I had joined in it.

The picture, at first sight, was not the same scene at all, of the laboratory that we had seen at the beginning of the experiment. And then, on second sight, it was too much the same, but in a most fantastic fashion.

We seemed to be looking outwards from the interior darkness of a cave.

I can only describe the scene in detail. It was the crucial piece of evidence and the subject, I suddenly realized, of what everything else, my own presence there, and that of General Bridger, and Reckman, and the Secretary and the Senator, was all about.

The picture, that could only have been actually taken by the camera, was a view outwards over tumbled rocks and debris. The outer wall of the laboratory, if it was the laboratory, was gone. The rock-face was open. And outside, beyond the wreckage, was a glimpse not of the hills around Lake Valley, but of ice-peaks, high and far away, and jagged mountains.

That was what the first glance showed. The second showed that there was something all too familiar about the cave. The rocks and debris in the foreground, though they were dark in the camera picture, had very much the look of the barrier wall. Jagged scraps glinted among them that could have been remaining fragments of the mirrors. There were items visible here and there in the cave that were certainly not rocks and certainly not natural. They had very much the look of being broken electrical equipment.

But the most important thing was shown almost clearly in the half-light from the entrance. It was the wrecked control desk, tilted and turned over, damaged as though something heavy had fallen on it from above, but none the less there.

And beside it, all too clearly in that inanimate scene, was a human skeleton.

The picture did not change. It just remained on the screen before us as the camera had gone on recording it until, as Galbraith told us, it had run out of film. For the camera, clock and instruments remained far longer on "the other side" as it was only possible to call it, than they were actually away from the laboratory.

But Galbraith did not tell us that. As we all sat silent in the dark projection room he began to tell us other things.

"It was a pity that Sara Francis saw these pictures when we first took them," he said quite quietly, speaking to us from the place he had taken at the end of the first row of the rank of chairs. "We had no idea, when we first took them, that we were going to get a scene like this. We had no idea when we took the first dark pictures we were going to get a skeleton. And we had no idea until we took these last good ones that we were going to be able to confirm that it was hers."

13

I felt a sudden impulse of horror. Sitting there, looking at that screen-picture, and listening to Galbraith, I all but disbelieved it. I thought of the girl I had just been talking to, not much more than an hour ago, and her vivid life and youth and enthusiasm as she worked and talked with Strassen. But Galbraith was inexorable. We could guess that in his mind there was nothing that could be left to chance.

"We had to tell her too, you see," he said. "We had to say why we wanted the X-ray photographs of her, to compare them with the skeleton. She herself is intelligent. She had to see for herself, to save us from lying as she called it. She doesn't know quite all of it. She hasn't the medical knowledge to compare the absence of thickening of those nasal bones in the skull with herself as she is today. She knows that that can't be a picture of her skeleton taken when she's very old. But she doesn't know how accurately we can say that if she is going to become like that, and therefore if this disaster, this cataclysm is going to happen all around the laboratory, it must be within a year or two, or probably much, much sooner."

We had been paralyzed, not only I but the civilians present and perhaps even General Bridger, by the disastrous picture on the screen and what Galbraith was saying about it. But the Senator got his breath.

"For God's sake!" he said. "You have that, you actually have that picture, taken out of a camera from your synchrotron, and you mean you still have that girl around here? Get her out! You don't mean you still let her into the laboratory?"

The Senator sounded as though he expected the synchrotron, the university, and all Lake Valley, to blow up at any moment. I think we all felt that. It was, after all, a camera picture. And the skeleton, if it had been proved to be Sara Francis, and a young Sara Francis, was damning. It was a threat, something more than a threat, that was beyond all believing.

"Wait!" Galbraith said. "I called you here to this confer-

14

ence on the assumption that we had to act. But do what? This is a scientific phenomenon and we can only approach it scientifically. We can only aim to find out more. And we have found out a little more already."

"Find out, hell!" the Senator roared. "Get everyone out! Close down that synchrotron! And clear the area!"

Galbraith went on, not the voice of sweet reason exactly, but deliberately, doggedly and obstinately. He went on just as though the Senator had not spoken.

"You see the first question is whether this is the future," he said. "It's hard to see how we can find that out, the status and nature of the observation, and whether or not it is some kind of illusion, unless we send a man. But suppose it is the future. As a hypothesis we have supposed it. A few things follow. That control desk in the picture is fairly clear. It's possible to work on the basis of the visible tarnish of the metal parts and other things. You might say that if it is the future then this picture was taken, if "was" is the word, about a hundred years ahead from now."

"You're mad, Professor," said Secretary Stephens softly.

"Not mad," said Galbraith, concluding in the darkened room. "Just doing what I always have done, which is to apply my intelligence to what we have. This picture is taken a hundred years from now. The disaster it records, on the face of it, is going to happen within the next few months. And it isn't local. Just look at that mountain chain outside the cave. But it won't happen today, tomorrow. That skeleton coincides with X-ray pictures of Sara Francis quite exactly except in one particular. If you look carefully at the slightly shadowy picture of the lower jaw, you'll see there is just one tooth missing. Not broken. Dentistry. A clear and neat extraction. But in life today, Sara Francis still has that tooth. She's safe, I think. We're all safe, just until she has a toothache. But when she feels she has to have that tooth out, then everything shown in this picture, we can only assume, is due to happen at any minute. That will be the time to take precautions. But as for closing the synchrotron down, Senator,

15

I think on the contrary we will have to use it to its maximum extent, and find out what we can, and act before then."

He concluded on a deliberate and almost savage note of logic.

II

I HAD STOOD stunned in the familiar office. Through the window I could see the hangar, the building with the centrifuge machine, and the distant sight of the rocket pads. It was the office in which they told us the results when we had been through one of those physical or mental stress-sessions in the course of which they had more means of instilling terror, we said, than had ever been known to man.

It was in that office too that they told those of us who had failed, when their hopes and ambitions were suddenly at an end and they were out. But I had not expected that to happen to me.

"What did I do?" I said. I was trying to understand it. "How do I know there's not been some mistake? Where did I fail? In what? If it was that acceleration test last night . . ."

The Colonel looked at me steadily across his desk. He was accustomed to dealing with men in a state of emotion without feeling it himself.

"I have a right to know!" I said.

"You did not fail," he said.

I stood there dumbly. To me it seemed that there was treachery in the world around me.

"You have been appointed to other work," he said.

I did not believe he could do it. He could, of course. A man does not sign on to become an astronaut and fly among the stars. He signs on to do what he is told and to go to where he is sent. But I was one of the few who had set my faith in this. I had believed in it, aimed for it, from the beginning. And I had thought I was getting there.

"I wish to resign my commission," I said. "I will leave the service."

"You will think about that again," he said.

"It should be understood," I said. "A man endures so much. If he does not fail, he has a right to know that his attainment, his sacrifice, depends only on himself."

"Do you want me to tell you about your new work?" he said.

"No."

He gave me a sealed envelope. "It's in there," he said. "As much as can be told to you about it before you actually get there. That's all, Major Judgen."

He dismissed me. As I turned to go, he said,

"I'm sorry, Howard."

I went on out. He could be sorry. He would sit at that desk for ever and a day sending other men into space, but at least he had that much connection with the rocket program, while I was out.

I packed quickly. We always did that. When one of us was dropped from the flight program he packed and got out quickly while the others were still at work. He just disappeared. It was better than meeting to say good-bye. There was too much feeling on either side, and it happened far too often.

It was like cutting off a limb.

I was in the car before I knew what I was doing. I was in it and rolling down the highway before I realized that I did not know where I was going. I had no home to go to. I was one of the few men who were unmarried, and that, I guessed, must have counted against me both ways, both because they preferred the stability of married men and because I had no dependents or others to suffer at my change of location and change of job. But that was later thought. Just then I was driving up the highway and it came to me as an academic thought that I might be driving in the wrong direction.

I pulled in to the side of the highway and opened the envelope I had been given.

Report to:

> Prof. T. Galbraith,
> Nucleonics Faculty,
> Proton-synchrotron Laboratory,
> Lake Valley University,
> Lake Valley, Tennessee,

the instructions read.

I opened the flap of the envelope again and tipped it, waiting for whatever else would come out in the shape of travel orders, time-schedules, ancillary instructions, or explanations. There was nothing. I squeezed the envelope open and looked in it.

I was on my own. I was not even told how, when, or by what route, I should arrive. They could leave it, naturally, to a man in my position. They may even have thought, 'He has a car. He will have his limited serviceman's belongings in the car. It will be easier for him to drive there.' But they did not usually do that. They had ways of studying the individual, but they were not those ways. When I was posted to Canaveral, I was ordered to fly there, and it was left to me to collect my car the next time I had time available in the shape of leave, or to have it sent on as freight. With some of us, in our service, they had cultivated an almost deliberate blindness.

To hell, I thought. I could go on a blind. I could disappear for a week or two. After being tensed up for so long, it was a big temptation.

Instead, I started the car and drove on to the nearest town. I found a hotel and used their hall. I had them put through a person-to-person call to Professor T. Galbraith and tell me when they got him. I sat waiting in the lounge. I was going nowhere. Maybe the 'they' who ran my life, having selected me for one job, knew exactly what I would do.

"Professor T. Galbraith?" I said to the phone. "This is a

Major Howard Judgen. I've been told to report to you. Just when exactly do you want me?"

The voice at the other end took me in its stride. He might have been arranging delivery for a refrigerator or a cooker.

"Tomorrow, Major? Can you make it at least by Thursday?"

He spoke of me as about some item of equipment that he would be needing shortly and intended soon to use.

"So soon?" I said.

"I don't mind, Major." He seemed surprised. "But don't you think you'd better look at it before you risk your neck for us?"

III

WE WERE STANDING in an illuminated rock tunnel, deep-hewn in the cliff-face below the hillside. We were far back from what I understood to be the business end of the proton-synchrotron, at what they called the start-end of the linear accelerator, in air-conditioned chambers underground, when the red-headed young man called William Strassen put his hand on my arm.

"This is almost the classic case of scientific discovery, Judgen. You have to know what is involved to understand it. You have to know of what his greatness consists. In Galbraith's case it was a question of his position, as chief and mentor of all of us here, and his status as a scientist. He was endowed with a research tool costing a hundred million of the Government's money. But that was not enough. That was a beginning. The time came when the research tool, all this that you see here, these excavations, the synchrotron, the hydro-electric generators producing power enough to feed a major town, and all to his design, just did not function. You see? A lesser man would have acted in a state of panic. He would have said, with so much money already spent, and so much expected of us, let's do something, anything, to make it work. But not Galbraith. He stood in the big, shielded underground laboratory that you'll see down there. He said "So this is new. There is some principle here that we do not fully understand. Keep everything as it is and launch a program. The interesting thing is just why it does not work."

I had arrived at Lake Valley the night before, driving up the winding valley road and seeing the university buildings tinted pink in the evening sunlight on the hillside. I had not known what it was at the head of the valley and had had no idea it was connected with the university. I had thought it was a power station with the big conduits bringing down water for the hydro-electric power, and that the rest had something to do with industry. I did not know a research tool could be so big. I had no acquaintance with a proton-synchrotron.

Strassen was Galbraith's chief research assistant. And Sara Francis, hovering around him in her long white coat, looked at him earnestly.

"Tell him," she said. "Tell him what it meant to a man of Galbraith's reputation that a hundred-million-dollar research tool that he had designed, and for which atomic scientists throughout the world were waiting, was standing idle. Tell him how they said he was incompetent and should never have been given the project in the first place, and how Galbraith stood firm and said, 'There is a basic scientific principle here, and something far more fundamental to be discovered with all this machinery failing to do what it is designed and supposed to do, than we could ever hope to discover if it were working and firing its particles at target atoms and performing such little tricks as turning lead to gold.' "

I looked at what they called the proton feeder source in the hewn rock tunnel, and at the great array of conduits and sectioned tubes and cables that led away in straight-line

20

diminished distance towards the proton-synchrotron housing at the far end. I said,

"Just how?"

They wore puzzled expressions, turning to look at me almost suspiciously, unable to believe that I could be so stupid, so I told them, "Galbraith tried to tell me after the man who met me here took me to him last night. He was too advanced for me. As soon as he began to talk about this I could not understand him."

They looked dubious and led me to the proton feeder source, which I understood was designed to create a rarified ion cloud at the end of the long white tube that ran the length of the tunnel in a sequence of jointed sections.

"You know what a proton is?" Sara Francis said impatiently. She treated me at high school level for a moment. "The nucleus of a hydrogen atom?" Then she looked at me inquisitively, smiled momentarily and turned her impatience on herself: "We use protons as the fundamental particle, as the missile of our research tool. In effect this is a gun to shoot them forwards."

William Strassen put his hand on my arm again and began to lead me down the tunnel towards the synchrotron.

"We are following the route the protons travel." He showed me section after section of the tube. "These forces are all exerted on their tiny object. The protons are attracted forwards by a charge that passes just ahead of them like the curl of a breaking wave. They fall. They fall through an electro-static field that has the power of a hundred million volts. Each section of this tube is an accelerator in itself."

"A hundred million volts exerted on the proton's tiny mass," Sara Francis said, "gives an answer that begins to approach the speed of light."

Ahead, the tube passed through a barrier that hid its destination. We went round the barrier by steps and a passageway in the rock. We came out into a chamber or curving tunnel. To right and left the ends bent away and it was obvious that, deep underground, they would meet to form a perfect circle. It was not a tunnel in effect, but a great hall with something massive in the centre.

The proton tube entered through the barrier and ran into a metallic housing that curved around the centre.

"This is where the power goes," Strassen said. "The power to run a town. It's not exaggerating to say that this is the world's most powerful magnetic core." He indicated the massive center with its coils and windings. "Our proton is like a flying electric current. We guide it in its path by magnetic forces."

"There is a limit to electrical insulation," Sara Francis said. "There is a limit to what can be achieved by a linear accelerator in a straight drop. But here the protons are circling in a spiral. We give them an impulse each time they come round and make them move faster still."

They were enthusiasts. They must have worked on that synchrotron from the beginning and they showed it to me as though it was their baby. I saw objections in my ignorance. To them it was a passion.

"I thought you said your protons were already travelling at near the speed of light. If I remember anything of Einstein at all, he says that that is the ultimate, that nothing could ever travel faster. Or if it did, in some fashion I can't explain, its transit would be instantaneous and it would be everywhere at once."

They looked at me suddenly as though I had cheated them in some way, standing in the echoing hall within the rock.

"Other people do it," said William Strassen sharply. "The European proton-synchrotron at Geneva has a final output of twenty-five thousand-million volts!"

"And yours?" I said. "What's yours—all this—designed to do?"

"Two point five million million volts!"

"There is a difference?"

"Just a hundred times as much," Sara Francis said as though that were nothing, but confronting me no longer as though I were a child.

"Theirs works, yours doesn't?" I said. I looked around at the great rock dome and massive windings. I believed I could see why there was a limit to the size of these things, even if they couldn't. And I was prejudiced by what I had already heard. They had built all this, and instead of the hardest atom-smashing rays ever, nothing, just nothing, came out at the end.

"You've got this wrong, Judgen," Strassen told me seriously. "It isn't that we reach a limit at the speed of light, which is what you're thinking. Physical particles can never reach the speed of light. They begin to gather size and mass. The Russians are already using these more massive particles to bombard their targets in a point five million-million synchrotron at Novorosisk."

He had calmed and become firm and clear. For a young man he was strangely, mentally, formidable. I realized he knew what he was talking about if ever anyone did.

And as for me, it was true what the girl had thought. I was no more than a visitor in their great rock halls. In their particular subject I was a child in arms.

They took me on to their laboratory. It was, as they said, the business end, in a great rock chamber. The protons should have come out there, flying out through a slit tangentially, and the laboratory was divided into two halves, a safe area behind a barrier wall, and an unsafe area filled with robot machinery around the target, that we could only view through mirrors. In the safe area where we stood was a control desk from which, I learned, Sara Francis controlled the operation of the synchrotron, while the effect of high-speed protons on the target was watched and recorded through instruments of fantastic delicacy, in theory, by Strassen and Galbraith or whoever might be the other operators allowed the use of the machine when once they got it going.

"So what is the answer?" I asked Strassen while I looked around the spaces of the laboratory where students were working on apparatus and where one side was mirrors that showed us the "hot" area, which was even deeper in the rock. "What is the cause of your trouble, since Galbraith told me that when you're working the synchrotron near its maximum, and you should be getting a beam of particles striking that target behind the wall there, you get nothing out at all?"

"Not nothing," said Sara Francis.

Strassen looked at me strangely.

"The insulation breaks down," he said.

"You mean you get a spark?"

He looked at a student who was working near us, then moved me away from him. It was a deliberate gesture. He took me to a little table, and we bent over it, looking at some scraps of metal that had been removed from round the target and that were looking strangely aged, and crystaline and powdery around the edges.

"The time insulation," he said. "What else? We're working very near the edge of things. Who knows what happens when a solid particle is speeded up ever nearer to the speed of light and begins to increase in size and mass?"

It was Sara Francis who told me quietly.

"We know, we believe, that we get an effect in time," she said. Across the table with its exhibits she looked at me steadily with her intelligent, frank gray eyes. "We did not know at first. We tried to record the passage of the protons, or some kind of radiation, on photographic plates. The proton beam should have punched holes right through them. Instead, we had to put in a camera to get anything at all. And then, instead of a record of the halo we thought that we were seeing, we got strange pictures."

I looked back at the mirrors as though I might see something there in the inhuman, forbidden area beyond the wall.

"Pictures?"

"What do we know," said Strassen, "about these strange regions where particles are approaching the speed of light? Each bigger synchrotron that is built brings solid matter nearer to a state that is unattainable and impossible. You know that, Judgen? If a particle did travel at the speed of light it would transit instantaneously. It would be in two places simultaneously and everywhere at once. It's size and mass would then be infinite so it would be everywhere before it even started. Something must break down before then. There is always something that happens before you touch infinity. But there are only a limited number of parameters in a field equation, and the one that cracks is time."

IV

GENERAL BRIDGER was convinced by the time the lights came on.

"Come," he said to myself and Reckman. He took us out to sit in his car.

We went out of the building and got into it. The General took the wheel himself. He dismissed his man. But he did not turn the engine or shift the ignition switch. We just sat there, I beside him in the front seat and Reckman in the back.

When the General did not say anything, but sat there as though he were driving at high speed to nowhere, Reckman began to talk methodically, not saying anything it seemed, but going over the points we already knew.

"We know it's impossible," he said in his flat voice. "In the laboratory they ended the experiment at half past twelve. In the view taken from the camera in the bell-jar, the laboratory clock was showing twenty of three by the time we lost it. By then, the bell-jar and its contents had been sent, had taken all those pictures and come back. The experiment had been dismantled. The camera had been taken out of the bell-jar and the film taken from the camera. Yet the record was taken of a time when the camera was not there. All right. There was consistence. The clock and the recording instruments when they recovered them showed an elapsed time of eight hours ten minutes. There is a logic within a logic. The pictures may be genuine. Or the Professor may be giving us a line of hocus-pocus."

The General sat for a while in the car, then turned to me. "What's your impression, Judgen? You're new and fresh to this. The Professor's synchrotron won't work. So he produces all these pictures. Do you think he's bluffing?"

He meant me to think before I answered, and so I did that.

"You've found a motive, sir," I said, looking straight ahead. "If the synchrotron was out of action for some design-fault reason, he could be tempted to make up something to clear his name. There is that. But I don't see him doing it. I've seen him, I've listened to him. To my mind he's the kind of man who, if there was anything about his equipment he did not know, he'd call someone else in even if it was the nearest plumber. He'd only be interested in finding out. He'd think about his name afterwards. And then there are the other facts that make his position unimpeachable and quite certain."

"What facts?" the General said.

"Sara Francis and William Strassen," I said.

"They're in the plot?" said Reckman.

"Not in a million years and ten thousand cataclysms and disasters," I said.

The General went on sitting there. I wondered what he thought of me.

Reckman after all had his job to do. It was his business to be suspicious. It was that kind of job. I never wanted it.

"There have been famous scientific frauds," he said. "Like the case of the Piltdown Man."

Bridger turned to him and said: "Drop it, Reckman."

So we began to think again. I did. The General had apparently finished thinking.

He began talking to me.

"You know the competition is keen for the space-ride, Major. You might just go back there someday. You aren't dismissed from that work. It was just that we needed someone. You were riding fairly high. You might have got a flight in a time or two. But your whole background is taken into consideration, for instance whether you volunteer for things or not. But this isn't like that."

"Sir," I said.

"What I mean is that you don't have to volunteer," he said.

I thought about it. It was hard to believe in that range of mountains that had shown in the photographs. They had looked unreal, like the Himalayas. I found my thoughts turning to Sara Francis. She was real. I wondered about William Strassen and whether he was married, and just what it meant to two people to work together on a thing like that, and what a stranger could do to cut him out.

"I volunteer," I said.

General Bridger grunted. Later, when I knew him better, I found he did that in a bar when anyone put a glass before him, or at meals when anyone put food on his plate.

"Congratulations," said Reckman dryly.

"Let's go," the General said. He began to drive the car down in the direction of the laboratory and the synchrotron.

"It could be an atomic war," he said on the way. "The question is if even an atomic war is big enough to create the situation that is visible in the cave. Or it could be a local disaster. If it's a local disaster, the Senator's right. We'll have to clear the area. But if it's an atomic war the question is who hit us. With this instrument we may get advance warning. We can do more than that. We can get our own blow in first."

I turned round in the seat and Reckman looked at me uneasily. I looked back at him. We both felt there was some doubt about the General's analysis, but we did not know what. We did not speak.

Down at the synchrotron we called for Strassen and Sara Francis. They met us, Strassen coming forward. It seemed he had heard of the General and his connection with the affair, but not actually met him. I performed the introductions.

"We have decided to send a man," the General said. It was not strictly true. Galbraith and the Senator and the

FIRST THROUGH TIME

Secretary were still arguing about it, and all they could be arguing about was a recommendation that would have to go elsewhere. But the General had decided and Strassen seemed to accept that. He nodded.

"Just how can we send a man?" the General said. "What do you need? What help can we give you? It may take time for agreement to come through, but we can get everything prepared and ready. We can begin now, and then, when the word comes, we can go."

I thought Strassen might make objections to the pushing, aggressive service way. I knew that handling the synchrotron was not like loading a gun and pulling the trigger and firing it. But he took it well and told the General "Come!" and led us into the workings.

They had a small work room with apparatus-assembly benches adjacent to the laboratory, and he took us to that. There was just room for us amid the various items of apparatus and instruments in process of construction but Strassen took us to the main bench where an intricate and beautiful machine was being made and already half finished.

Its basis was a large transparent sphere of hard plastic, about four-feet-six in diameter but at present, open on the bench and divided into two halves. Mounted in the lower half already was a mass of intricate apparatus, a battery power pack and a series of electric eyes and instruments all mounted on a metal sub-frame. But already in pride of place in the completed framework was a complicated camera with a turret of different lenses and machinery to change them and tilt and pan the camera and alter aperture and focus.

"What is it?" the General said.

"Our robot observer," Strassen said. "Able to illuminate and focus on every detail of the cave. More than that. Able to turn an astronomical telescope lens on the night sky outside the cave and take records that will tell us exactly when the pictures are being taken: the date and season of the year while registering climatic and every other kind of data. This plastic sphere itself," he tapped its hard and glass-like surface, "is designed to take advantage of the maximum vol-

28

ume of material the synchrotron can handle. If you insist on sending a man, then all you have to do is take all the machinery out and put in a seat or whatever else you think you need to make a human observer comfortable."

His voice was cold and he was looking at the General. His attitude was restrained and remote, I thought, and distinctly lacking in that enthusiasm of which I knew him capable. The General saw it too.

"You say if we *insist* on sending a man?" he said.

"Your man isn't going to take observations as accurately as this machine," said Strassen.

"A man can get out of the sphere and climb over the rocks and see what's outside the cave!" the General said.

"What for?" said Strassen.

We were all standing crowded before the bench and we had been examining the machine, but now we were looking at the two of them and they were the only ones who were talking.

It was a conflict of temperament largely, I realized, between Strassen whose approach was scientific, who wanted observations mostly, and to whom they were most real, most valid and useful, when they consisted of accurate photographs and graphs on paper, and the General who wanted action. But it was something more than that.

"Dammit, man, this isn't just an academic scientific experiment! It isn't detailed photographs of the cave we want, but to know whether it is really there or not, and if so if that damned new mountain chain is there outside it or if it's an illusion! If it's true, we've got to know that as soon as possible and see what we can do about it!"

"That's what I mean," said Strassen. "You can't do anything."

The General stared as though Strassen were some raw recruit who had not yet been taught that the army did not know the meaning of *impossible*.

"As you say," Strassen said, "you want to know whether the cave of which we have pictures is true or not. You mean you want to know whether it is the future or not. But if it isn't the future, you don't need to bother. You don't need to do anything about it because in that case it isn't so. But if it is the future, you can't do anything about it. The fact that you could alter it in any way would prove it was not the future."

"Metaphysics!" the General said.

"Not so," said Strassen. "Just logic. If these pictures we've got, of a disaster in our laboratory that has become a cave, do represent the future, then so far as they are concerned whatever we are doing now has already happened. They mean that the future is there; it's fixed, it's final, emerging out of some causation that took place in our present and its past. The future must be like that if the scientific presumption that every event must have a material cause is true. The theory of causation implies determinism. It means that whatever you do now, no matter what you do, must contribute to the future as it's going to be. No matter what you do now, your actions must be part and parcel of the creation of that future. It must be so or there would be no logic and no science. We would have events happening in the present that were not caused and had no connection with anything in the past. The answer would be chaos."

Strassen had paled slightly. He did not find it easy to stand up to the General. But his dictum was staggering in its implications. It was as staggering as the youthful assumption of intellectual superiority with which he put it to the General. Yet Reckman saw his point. It was the thing he and I had been doubtful about when the General had been talking of using the synchrotron as a kind of advance-warning air-raid alert system, when we were arriving in the car. He came in quickly:

"You mean if the synchrotron were capable of showing us pictures of a catastrophe as a warning, and we were capable of averting the catastrophe, then the synchrotron wouldn't be showing us pictures of a catastrophe in the first place?"

"Exactly," Strassen said with the chilly, daunting smile of the man of intellect confronted by the men of action. "I told you: the past causes the present, the present causes the future. That is the basic, fundamental assumption of science. It is determinism, maybe. But the only difficulty about prediction, as any scientist will tell you, is just that we don't know enough. That's why we study. But that's what we should do about this, and all we can do about this. Study it! See what we can learn from it! And with all due respect, it's only a General who would think of taking short cuts!"

I watched General Bridger. I was alarmed. I knew that a General, by the time he had risen to the rank and seniority of Bridger, must have some experience of dealing with civilians. But with top civilians and the higher politicians, and then not without, as history showed, a considerable degree of friction. But for him to be confronted by a civilian of Strassen's youth and lack of status, and to be taunted with an assumption of intellectual superiority in just that way, might produce an explosion, I thought, at any moment.

Bridger behaved well. At least he kept the remnants of his dignity. If he went red it was no more than could be expected. "Strassen," he said, "You're under orders! You aren't in charge here. Fortunately, that's Galbraith. But if you were, you'd learn some elementary facts. You'd learn that when I say we send a man, then we send a man!"

"I didn't say we wouldn't, did I?" Strassen said. "So far as I remember the reason we came in here was because you wanted me to show you how to do it in the first place."

The event was smoothed over in that way and we went on to talk about whether I should be fitted with a space-suit and oxygen cylinders and other equipment, and if so how we would fit them in the sphere. But Reckman and I had a word about it when we found ourselves together as we came out.

"The young man had a point," he said, looking at me curiously as we went towards the cars. "Suppose this is the future, this place you're going, and the General succeeds in altering it on the basis of your report when you come back, just where exactly, and what should we call it, the place where you have been?"

"I know," I said. "I don't like it. If I go there, and then come back, and then we alter it, it won't only be that the place and situation where I've been won't exist any more. We will have created events that will imply that not only does it not exist but it never will exist and has never been. But the General's right, you know. He's had more experience of human limitations, especially of knowledge, then Strassen. The only thing to do is try it."

V

In what little time I had left to me before I went, I did my utmost to get to know Sara Francis.

I suppose it was natural I should feel for her. Everyone did. Hers was a situation no girl, no human being, had ever met before. It was not merely that there was in existence a photograph of what purported or appeared to be her skeleton after death. That was taken, so far as any of us could guess, at a period of a hundred years on, and almost all of us then living would be skeletons by then. It was more the particular circumstances of the photograph, the fact that it was the skeleton of Sara as a young woman, and not Sara old, and all the surrounding detail, the disaster in the working laboratory of the synchrotron, the wrecked control desk, and all the other evidences of some vast and near disaster in the place where she went on working. It was true there was the singular item, the saving detail of the tooth, on which Galbraith placed his confidence, insisting on its abolute validity, but it was an incredible situation to be hanging over anyone, and I was surprised, even shocked and a little awed, that she bore up so well.

I went walking with her in the evening along the pathways the students had made that led along the valley sides and into the woods. We had been busy all day with the preparations, but when I asked her what she was doing in the evening, she was free. I was wrong about her and Strassen. They worked together, but even before she met him he had been happily married.

"Why don't you go away?" I asked her. "It's hard to see how it could happen, the situation in the wrecked laboratory, if you just went to live somewhere else, a hundred or a thousand miles away, and never came near this place again. I don't think anyone would blame you. I don't see how they could. And despite Galbraith, it might even be the most sensible thing, as a precaution, for all of us."

We were walking along the path at that time towards the woods, and she glanced at me.

"Do you think I should do that? Do you want me to?"

"No," I said. "I'd like to say yes. My feelings tell me to say yes. But while you still have that tooth, I think Galbraith's right. I don't see how you can get round that fact. I'm being selfish."

She grinned at me cooly in inquiry, teasing me a little, wondering which way to take it.

It was true that one of the reasons Galbraith wanted to keep her there if we were to send a man was that it would be safer for me. It was not easy to understand what was happening with the synchrotron, and there were numbers of unknowns. No one knew exactly why, for example, the transfer was always to the cave at what appeared to be about the same time. They had tried it often enough, and got the same results, but with a new operator, who might unknowingly set up a slightly different field, no one knew what would happen. But that was not what I had meant when I said it, and she guessed it.

"So you want me to stay in preference to going to live a thousand miles away?"

"A thousand miles is a long way to go visiting," I said.

Her smile was still cool and challenging, almost a grin.

33

"And it might not be worth it, anyway," she said, "if I was the kind of girl who would want to cut up and run at the first sign of trouble instead of staying as long as possible to see what I could do about it."

I looked at the tops of the trees ahead, which were gilded in the evening light while the sun made long slanting shadows below them.

"Is that what you feel about it?" I asked her. "That you want to stay as long as possible and fight back—as long as you have that tooth?"

"It's a perfectly good tooth," she said with some indignation. "I never even had a toothache." Then she answered my question. She had that kind of mind. To her, questions were neither all gallant nor rhetorical. "I talked about it to Strassen too," she said. "I'm not in love with him, but I am influenced by him."

"What did he say?"

"Can't you guess? He said either this thing is a prediction, or it isn't. If it is a genuine prediction, no matter how, then it is absolute and final. We can't do anything about it, no matter how we try. But if it isn't a prediction, if we admit that anything we can do can change it, then it simply isn't a genuine picture of the future, and therefore there is nothing to worry about. Either way—he found it hard to say this, but he's a very honest man, Strassen—it was no good my attempting to run away."

I walked with her, feeling her companionship and wanting it, but at the same time thinking of Strassen's reasoning.

"That's a very masculine way of thinking," I said. "That kind of hard 'either, or' logic. It isn't the kind of thing that would normally appeal to a woman."

"People who don't believe in logic don't work with big and dangerous machines like a synchrotron," she said simply.

I got it then. It was the kind of revelation that comes sometimes in a lifetime. It isn't easy to explain. I had been proud, I suppose, without knowing it, in my work at the rocket base. Staking our lives on logic was our strength. We dealt with unimaginable forces. We faced heat, explosion, the vacuum and cold of space. We guarded against all contingencies, and because we were as near perfect as it was humanly possible to be, we got it right. We lived. Or if we failed, we died.

Now I realized that a girl in a laboratory could take as many risks, could calculate even more insidious forces than those we dealt with more precisely, and in short had my own brand of courage with far less show.

"All right," I said. "But in this case even if it were a prediction, I'm with the General. I think we can do something about it. Suppose this is a prediction. Suppose it's an actual picture of the future. The very fact that we have seen it changes things. We see it, therefore you go away. Some other events may happen, but not exactly that situation in the cave. The future has to alter! We make it so."

She walked with me a little way. We entered the woods and we stopped there in the cool lengthening shadows of the golden evening. She leant against a tree.

"Do you think so, Howard?" she said. "Do you think I haven't thought of that? Suppose I did go away. Suppose we trained a new operator and you used him or her when you made your attempt at a human transit. It's tricky, this thing that's happening with the synchroton. There are some mistakes an operator could make that would result in you getting not a time effect but a proton beam. You could be killed. But there are worse mistakes than that. Suppose instead of putting you down in the cave, in the wrecked laboratory, which is the one point in the future with which we have established certain contact, they dropped you in space somewhere, or they got you out there and could not get you back!"

I said nothing. There were dangers, we all knew, but no one had put them to me quite so clearly and bluntly as she was doing then. I wondered why.

But she stood looking at me with clear, frank look in her gray eyes.

"That's the trouble about prediction, Howard!" she said. "If it is a prediction, if it's a true prediction, it will be bound to happen. Don't you see? Do you think I haven't

35

thought of it? This new operator they would have to use if I went away: he could so easily get into trouble and get you away but not be able to bring you back. And then what would happen? What could they do but send for me? And what could I do but come back, if I heard they were in trouble? It would be like a nightmare. I don't like nightmare situations. I would come back and take over an experiment that was already in difficulties, a situation that was out of control! Who knows what would happen then? It would be something—it would have the inevitability of an old Greek tragedy! A situation already out of control and getting more out of control. No! I prefer to handle it from the start in a way that I know that I can!"

We were close together and alone in the woods. She looked fragile but determined, with a power of mind and spirit I had not seen before in any woman.

"There's one thing about that," I said. "If you went away, you'd have to make up your mind not to come back. Not to come back whatever happened."

She looked away from me.

"I can't do that, Howard. You are doing this for me, aren't you?"

I put out my hand onto her arm and I saw her move as I touched her. She looked up at me quickly, almost afraid. We looked into one another's eyes for a moment and recognized what we saw there.

"After this is over," I said. "Sometime—when we both can go away." Our eyes met and held for a moment.

VI

THE EXPERIMENT was timed for noon. They always had timed the experiments for noon. It was a matter of avoiding any confusion about the clocks.

I stood there in the safe half of the laboratory. The place was almost crowded since the General and Reckman were present as well as Galbraith and Sara and Strassen. I was wearing a standard high-altitude flying suit, and General Bridger watched me as I adjusted the belts and flaps. He had decided to be present for the experiment himself, and it was a measure of the importance he attached to it.

"Are you ready for him to go, Strassen?" he said. He looked at Strassen, who was handling the target-area instruments and the handling machinery, as though he were some kind of young subordinate and assistant who was not wholly to be trusted.

I did not share his view. Strassen was against the man experiment, but once it had been accepted he had thrown himself wholly into it. He was completely engaged in the readings he was taking and the work that he was doing, and he answered the General shortly: "Hold yet!" In fact there was no one in whose hands I would rather be than Strassen's, except maybe Sara's.

I looked at Sara. She looked a little pale but was wholly absorbed in her work at the control desk. There were times, in "bringing up" the synchrotron, when it functioned normally as a synchrotron and they got the proton beam. They had to be sure they were past those points and that they had something perfectly stable, in terms of the field and phase-relationships, before I could be allowed to enter the danger area.

Galbraith watched the two of them. I was afraid that

they might have been thrown off by the presence of General Bridger and Reckman, as well as their usual assistants who were in the background; but Galbraith, Sara and Strassen had a professional's degree of concentration. Not even Bridger's assumption that he was in command upset them.

The laboratory clock on the wall stood at four minutes to the hour. There was an odd remark.

Galbraith looked at me briefly. "Pity you couldn't go combat-armed," he said. He glanced at the clock and then at Sara and Strassen as though he could tell just how far they had got by their attitudes and the expression on their faces. "Give him his final instructions, General."

"You will go and take the observations as you have been instructed. You will emerge and photograph the area immediately around the cave," the General said. "You will then get into the capsule to come back. We will take no chances this time." He looked at Galbraith. "What's this about going combat-armed?" he said.

Galbraith himself had warned us that I was not to try to carry any weapons. It was something due to the eddy-currents set up in any metal objects around the synchrotron by the magnetic fields set up by the massive magnetic core. Fire-arms were out, yet now he was regretting it. He had spent the previous night examining the films and still pictures again and I wondered what he had seen in them that none of us had seen before.

"Go," said Strassen. "I am ready now to go." His tense voice cut across us.

The General, Galbraith and I were still engaged in the last minute conversation. Galbraith shook his head. "It isn't very likely," he said. "Judgen, take a look around this laboratory and imprint on your mind everything that is here." But he turned away from us then. He glanced at Strassen. "Go," he said. "You're holding now." He turned to Sara, not speaking to her loudly. "Strassen says go," he said and waited.

"The field is steady now," Sara said without looking up from her infinite concentration on the instruments on her control desk. "If it holds another thirty seconds, then you can go."

Galbraith looked up at the laboratory clock, but he pulled out his watch as well.

"Good luck, Howard," Reckman said.

"If he obeys his instructions he'll be all right," General Bridger said.

"Go," Sara said in a quiet voice that was firm except for the slightest trace of a catch in it. "Good luck, Howard." She must have been carrying that last phrase, determined to say it, all through her concentration.

"Strassen?" said Galbraith.

"Go," said Strussen.

"Now," Galbraith said to me. "Go now!"

The laboratory clock said two minutes to.

We had rehearsed the next step. I looked at the barrier wall and the view we had across it through the mirrors. The plastic sphere or capsule was standing in the "hot" half of the laboratory with the lower half of it, in which a seat had been fixed, established firmly on a plinth. The upper half was held above it and nearby in the "hands" of some of the complex machinery that Strassen operated. There was a ladder up our side of the barrier wall. I went to it and ran up it.

The aim was to keep me in the "hot" side of the laboratory, where no one would normally go at all, for as short a time as possible. I got to the top of the wall and saw the machinery, the plinth, the sphere directly, no longer viewing them through the mirrors. I must have been receiving some slight stray radiation at that point despite all Sara's and Strassen's care, but a bridge had been established from the top of the wall by the ladder to the lip of the sphere. It would have been possible for me to go round the wall and then climb up into the sphere, but that, it had been decided, would have taken longer. I ran across the bridge in fact and got at once into the lower half of the sphere, which had been lead-lined. I was getting far less radiation then. It had been estimated that it would not harm me at all if the period I was in it was of the order of a minute.

Behind me, I could hear Galbraith, who was looking at his watch, begin to count: "One, two, three, four . . ." I looked back at the safe side of the laboratory and realized that I could see all of them, Galbraith, Strassen, Sara, the General and Reckman, in the mirrors. Only the clock on the laboratory wall above them could be viewed directly. I wondered what was going to happen. I cannot pretend that I was not afraid. I would have sat in the nose cone of a rocket in comparative certainty and comfort. This was new. "Goodbye, Sara!" I called. I told the rest: "O.K.!"

In fact the machinery around me, in the target area of the synchrotron, was already moving. The top of the sphere too had been lined with an internal framework on which slid lead-lined slides or curtains and it was essential to get it down on me, and have me enclosed from the radiation as soon as possible. Strassen had not waited for my signal. His handling machinery, controlled by the wheels and grips below the barrier wall, was swinging into action. I had not time to think then.

An arm swung over me handing me oxygen cylinders. No vacuum had been encountered by instruments in the course of the transfer, but pressure variations had been registered, and when a cage of mice had been sent they had come back suffering apparently from slight asphyxia. The General was taking no chances. He had ordered oxygen and a suit that, if necessary, could be pressurized. I had to stow and clip on the cylinders and adjust my face-mask and plug myself in. Then my roof, the upper half of the sphere, was coming down over me.

Working in face-mask and goggles now, I steadied it with my hands and eased it into position, making sure that the two halves mated. It enclosed me in darkness since the interior shields were drawn. I drew one back and looked out and put my hand to the aperture and made the thumbs-up sign. I could see them watching me from a distance through the mirrors. The laboratory clock said one minute short of twelve. Galbraith held up both hands to me. It was the signal for me to re-draw the shutter. I was enclosed inside and could see nothing.

I had one minute to wait. It was the minute we had given ourselves to allow for all contingencies. I was sitting in a tight-closed sphere and I could feel instruments and shelves around me. I switched on a little light that was operated from a battery pack. I had time to glance at the instruments and see that they were reading normal. One of them was a clock. I do not know what I expected. I expected it to speed up, I think.

At noon precisely I felt a sense of vertigo that abolished instantly all other sensations whatsoever.

VII

THE SENSATION was one of nameless horror.

I had met, and risen above, every kind of spinning and falling sensation and zero gravity. We had been chosen and trained at the rocket base for physical assurance and temperamental stability. I do not pretend to be a superman. But, sitting enclosed in that sphere while the whole universe became chaos it seemed to me from the moment the transfer started, I knew that I was being called upon to endure things that no man should be asked to endure. To say that I knew then why the mice that had been subjected to the transfer showed signs of asphyxia would be not quite true. I did not know anything. It was from the first a sensation that I could not breathe, and that stops most things. And with it came a sensation that I was being slowly rolled over in space in a most complicated and remorseless fashion and at the same time bent in another direction so that I would, if the process continued, be turned inside out.

We had had no idea that I would be subjected to these sensations. A plan had even been laid down for me about what I was to do as I sat in the sphere when the transfer started. I was supposed to switch on my little light, look at all my instruments, and record their readings in my log book. Then I was to open one of the shutters with which I was surrounded, look out through the transparent surface of the sphere, glance at my instruments again, and record what I saw and what the instruments said. It was to have been a methodical scientific investigation, and just the kind of thing that I, with my training, was supposed to be able to do. Yet right from the first, held in a paralyzed horror in which I was unable even to gasp, I knew it was utterly impossible. I could only endure in that particular nightmare sensation in which I could not even scream.

It is impossible to explain how I could have had a sensation of simultaneous light and blackness. Later, but only after I had arrived after what seemed an infinite age of endurance, I found that my light had gone out. It was those eddy currents probably, induced by the magnetic effects of the synchrotron, that had put unusual currents in the circuit and blown the bulb. But I did not know that then. As I have said, from the very first instant I did not know anything. It was only that I felt, that I hoped rather than knew, that all the stars I was seeing, and the bright lights and grave-dark shadows, and the sounds that echoed through my helpless and quite horrible vertigo, were subjective sensations, and products of my mind, and not a universe that had become a madhouse.

It was not only a physical sensation. From the first as I fell through that light-dark void, I knew I was in a far greater danger.

It had a physical cause maybe. No doubt Galbraith or some doctor could have explained it to me. It could have been those eddy currents maybe working down my nerve-paths and my ganglions and through the matrix of my brain. But I did not know that during that dreadful fall through a void that was my period in the sphere. If I knew anything, if I could have known anything, or thought at all during that endless period, it would have been something like this: that there were limits beyond which no man should ever be asked to volunteer and endure, and these were not limits of pain or physical peril but something more and worse than that, the dangers that might result in the total destruction of his personality and turn him out at the end as a different kind of man.

I did not even know I was sitting in the sphere any more. All I knew was that there was a danger that I would come out of whatever it was I was in not as myself, as what I believed to be a man of sense and courage, but as some helpless, weeping, drooling thing. It was that I had to fight. It was that I had to struggle against in some fearful and gigantic contest over a spiritual abyss.

And it went on. I had paid no great attention previously to just how long it took to make the transfer, of the sphere or of instruments, from the laboratory to the cave. It had not seemed greatly important, since I had thought I would just be sitting there and making observations and recording. Maybe I had thought of myself as a camera. We all had. There was no way we could have found out what it was I would have to endure. If we had sent even higher animals, apart from mice, it would not really have shown on them when they came out, for it was the very nature of the thing that the higher the man involved, and the more developed his nervous system, his sensitivity and his capacity for reaction, the worse it had to be. So all I knew, as the seconds passed, and then the minutes, and the lights became coloured, red, which indicated perhaps how the blood was beating in my brain, was that I might come out of it dead or maybe, what was present as a fear, a good deal worse.

It was a mercy when the sensations began to lessen as my breath-starved body and my blood-starved brain began to verge towards unconsciousness. It was a mercy and yet a greater peril, for I felt that if I did give in to it, if I did let myself go into that particular unconsciousness, I would never come out of it as myself again.

It was as though my mind and body were dispersed, and scattered in individual atoms all through the universe, and I had to hold it all together, hang on across the spaces of the void, and keep myself together as a coherent whole, or be lost for ever more.

There was one thought, one positive actual thought that was in my mind at some time. It was that this was not all, this transfer, this single outward journey if it could be called that. Somehow, sometime, I would have to get back.

VIII

THERE WAS DARKNESS and stillness, and I was me. I did not know I was in the cave. I still did not "know" anything. I was just sitting there, crouched in the sphere, as in a womb.

I was not aware that I had suffered any damage. I knew it was a danger. I knew I should not just be sitting there in total darkness. I must assert myself. I must make sure that I was me.

I put out a hand and felt the sphere around me. I could feel one of the anti-radiation shutters. I did not know it was a radiation shutter, but I drew it back.

I sat there seeing again. I could see a scene before me. At least I had not lost all my senses. I had seen it before. It was the cave.

After a time, a sense of satisfaction came to me. I had arrived.

So what should I do now? A little light was coming into the sphere now I had opened the shutter. I could see shelves around me, and a log-book, and instruments. Was I supposed to do something about them? Write in the log book and read the instruments? I began to move around in the sphere.

I pushed the top off. I stood up in the sphere, and then stepped out of it. I stood shakily on a rock-strewn ground. I took off my face-mask and goggles and oxygen cylinders and put them in the sphere. I stood looking at them. I should not have done that, I knew. Not right away. Perhaps I was not remembering very well as yet. It would come back in a little time.

I looked around me.

Yes, it was a familiar scene. I had seen it before. At least I had seen pictures of it. I was in a shadowy cave. Rocks were piled across it as a barrier, creating shadows, and there were more rocks towards the entrance. Also there was a skeleton.

I started towards the skeleton.

I stopped half way. Somehow I did not like that skeleton. I was afraid that it was going to be real. It was real. Everything was real. The rocks were hard and felt like rocks. In the silence of the cave they clattered when I moved. Yet it was not a complete silence. I could see signs of sunlight outside the cave, and a range of snowy mountains, and somewhere in the distance a bird was singing. I sniffed the air. That was the reason why I should not have taken my oxygen mask off at once. I should have tested the air first. Yet it smelled like normal air: cool perhaps, but dry and tingling, with less moisture than I would have expected inside a cave.

I was standing on the barrier of broken rocks that stretched across the cave between the sphere and the skeleton. I could see two more skeletons now, that could not have been seen from the sphere. I was supposed to do something. It was in my mind somewhere. I was supposed to do a series of slow, methodical things, minutely examining the scene around me, looking at all the machinery and electrical apparatus, and writing in the log book about its state.

It did not seem important somehow. I was primarily concerned with the skeleton, the first one, the one I had seen before taken in a picture by a camera. What mattered was whether it was actually there or not. What mattered was who it was, and whether I could actually see it, touch it, feel it. I took my courage and went to it.

I was feeling better then. I was feeling better all the time, though I had a long way to go before I was wholly normal. Yet crouching by that skeleton I felt sad somehow. It was too real. I put out my hand to touch it and two bones fell apart with a clatter. I have to be clear about this. My mind, my memories, were disordered. Yet that did not cloud my physical impressions and responses, but heightened them. Had there been anything wrong or false about any of my impressions, I would have felt it. Instead my sense had the clear, whole freshness of a child's. Things and the world are more real to a child than they are to an adult, just because he sees them directly and not through preconceptions, and so it was with me.

The whole situation I was in, the cave, the rocks, the smashed electrical equipment, the wreckage of the laboratory, the holes in the roof from which the rocks had come down, and the outer rock wall that had disappeared, were all clear to me in a kind of springtime freshness. And I took the skull of the skeleton in my hands and fondled it.

There was no mistaking the smooth, cool touch of actual bone. That sensation is as clear to me today as are childhood sensations which one remembers always and which are always more vivid than anything in adult life.

So, I thought, I had it in my hands. There was nothing I could do about it. It was there. I got up with it and took it back with me carefully, moving through the cave to the sphere, passing the broken control desk on the way.

I carefully put the skull in the sphere and picked up the upper half of the sphere with outstretched hands, to put it on. Then I chanced to see the log book on its shelf in the sphere.

I put down the top again and picked up the log book. I wrote in it, using the pencil that was clipped to the book and resting it on the upper half of the sphere as a table to write on.

"I am sending you the skull," I wrote. "I cannot come back at once. This journey is very bad. If I never come back and you send someone else, put him in an iron lung and give him sedatives before you send him."

I looked at what I had written. As I say, my mind had the simple clarity of a child. I doubt if I even knew who I was writing to. A million questions remained unanswered. There was no guarantee that if I let the sphere go back without me that day, and they sent it the next day from the laboratory, that it would arrive on the next day in the cave. It might arrive a year later or even earlier. But my mind was at that time incapable of dealing with such complications. I only knew, with satisfaction, that I was doing the best I could.

I put the log book back in the sphere and I put the skull upon it. Then I put the top back on. I felt that I had discharged my duty, the first things I was supposed to do, immediately on arrival.

Then I looked around the cave. Something was in my mind. Someone had said they wished I could go combat-armed. That implied that there could be a danger. I could not see any. The cave looked as still as if it had been like that for a hundred years. I had a memory of a voice saying to me "Take a look around the laboratory and imprint it on your mind." It was a memory that came to me because that, the ability to deal with clear, actual impressions, was something I had very much just then. I was very physical and actual, not less so than usual but more so, and I stood by the sphere, which I had closed in the deep, shadowy part of the cave, and looked about me and noticed the things a child would have noticed.

In the laboratory, in that position by the sphere, I would

have been surrounded by the robot handling machinery, consisting of metal bars and grips and an array of almost human arms and joints. I looked around for it. The natural assumption was that it had all been smashed and buried by the rock-falls. But I looked for it among the rocks, and it was not there.

I looked at the skeletons again then. None of them were clothed. It was a simple and obvious fact. It had been quite visible in the photographs. The clothing, we had all assumed, would have decayed away. But would it, both the natural and the man-made fibers, not leaving even a scrap?

I did not remark on things or note them with surprise. That was not my frame of mind. I just assumed, on the spot, and naturally, that other men had been in the cave before me, a long time ago. They had come before the bodies were skeletons; before they had decayed. They had come in a matter of days after the great catastrophe, and they had taken metal bars and clothing.

I went walking and climbing out towards the exit or entrance to the cave then. I was supposed to do something about that, too. But I was not going to take photographs and obey my orders. I went with a natural curiosity. I went to look.

I sat out in the sunlight in the entrance of the cave when I came to it. I sat on sun-warmed rock and my legs were dangling over a cliff. Something had happened to the valley. It was no longer the green and verdant Lake Valley that I knew. Instead, I was in a bare and rocky landscape that might have been among the mountains of the moon. The stony valley floor was two hundred feet below me, and the solid hillside of rock that I was on must have been lifted up and tilted backwards as had other rocks on the farther valley side. It was only because the great slice of rock had been lifted bodily that the cave was still intact. Nothing else was.

The valley was a great rocky canyon, with jagged mountainous hills on the other side. It was like a view of the earth after the mountains had been upraised but before the soil had formed. The country was inexplicably dry and barren, too, and it was only around the great snow peaks that rose beyond the nearer foothills that clouds were floating. There was rain, or rather snow there, for the hills were ice. Even the great conical volcano that was smoking there was iced except for a dark and grimy ice-free area just around its crater-peak. The stream that flowed down the valley, winding along a stony bed, must come from that source. It came out of the mountains and descended into the valley by waterfalls.

My eye followed the stream down, seeing how here and there, in the surrounding grandeur and desolation, it had encouraged little patches of green, only visible when one looked for them but significant of the way that life was coming back. They were more prevalent further down the valley, and I believed I could see creatures grazing on them, maybe mountain goats. My eye swept the scene, then my gaze fixed and held.

From behind a rocky outcrop, at some distance down the valley, I could see rising a single line of smoke.

People, I thought. No other creature made fire but man. And so they had survived then, those men who had come into the cave, searching desperately, and taken metal bars and clothing. Somehow, even among the sparse vegetation that was all that was left after the destruction of the soil, they had survived the cataclysm that had annihilated all their world.

Sitting there in the sunlight, and understanding all these things quite calmly, I came back to myself sufficiently to wonder what I was doing there.

I had been sent to find out what had happened, had I not? I had been sent to discover what I could by a process of scientific observation and detailed, logical thought that, although I was getting better and recovering from my journey, I did not feel I could undertake just then.

But there were men down there, and it seemed to me that the simple, logical thing to do was to go down and ask them.

IX

ACCORDING TO the clocks and the instruments that had been
sent before, the sphere would remain where it was in the
cave for about eight hours. I was remembering this now.
Little by little my mind was clearing and my memory was
coming back. I was thankful for this and I almost felt myself.
I had been lucky. There had been a balance about my mind
and about my personality that had brought me through intact. But I still did not want the strain of detailed technical
thought. Instead, it came to me that what I needed most
was a trip down into the valley.

The idea of walking and climbing, and maybe talking
instead of doing technical work and trying to think, seemed
to me so attractive as to be almost beautiful.

I looked about me for some way across the rocks around
me and down the sunlit cliff to the valley floor. There had
to be a way. The cave had been ransacked. It did not look
easy at first, but then I saw it. Below me and sideways,
there was a ledge. From the ledge it looked possible to
reach a gulley. The gulley led down, as a crack in the rock-
face, to the valley floor or at least to the great pile of
tumbled rocks that must have fallen away from the cliff
below me.

I got up and flexed my body in the sunlight. It felt all
right. I went to the extreme edge of the cave entrance
and started down towards the ledge.

I had been right. My mind, my whole being felt better
when I was climbing. I even believed I was better at it than
I would have been normally. I was less impressed than I

would have been at other times by the drop below me. I was full of confidence about little things, such as that a foot-hold or hand-hold that will hold you when three feet off the ground is equally good when you are hanging above space at two hundred feet. I worked out along the ledge.

I had trouble in the gulley. I admired those men who must have climbed that route a hundred years ago. They could not have been sure of what they were going to get when they got there. No more, I thought, was I. I swung round a point and over a chock stone. At the same time, I thought, it was important to survive.

It was easier when I reached the great scree or rock fall that sloped away down to the valley floor. It was no more than a matter of being careful that a rock did not turn under me as I leapt on it when going down the slope and cause me to break an ankle or give me a twisted leg.

It was hot in the sunlight. I unzipped my flying suit, but by the time I reached the valley bottom and was working along the stream, I realized I did not need it. I was wearing regular trousers and shirt and sweater underneath, and I took it off, looked around for a conspicuous rock, and stowed it away beneath it. I felt better then, but found myself looking at the stream and wondering if it were good to drink. It was certainly clear and had come down from the mountains. I did not know about radioactivity or other dangers. I found myself, in my better mental state now, try-ing to visualize the readings of my instruments as I had last seen them when I left the sphere. I hit something awkward there. I had a mental image of the radiation meter, and it seemed to me that when I had last seen it, it had been reading less than zero. Its needle had been hard back against the stop.

Negative radiation is an impossibility. I decided that that meter must have been affected by the transfer just as I had. It gave me a worry though. If my instruments had been affected by the transfer this time, then they must have been affected by it on other occasions, when they had been sent before. We had thought we knew there was no radioactivity or other dangers in the environment, but I was well aware by then that there was far too much we did not know.

All the same, I could not exist in that place and not breathe or eat or drink. I found a green patch by the stream, one of the first I had come to, and knelt by the clear water.

I drank, and then looked at the green herbage, that I thought was grass, that I was kneeling on. I looked at it slowly and then wished I had not drunk that water, or breathed that air or arrived in that place at all.

The "grass" was composed of tiny reed-like plants. Each one was different. Some had tiny flowers and some had none. But none of them was like any plant I had ever seen. Among all their short, close-matted diversity, I could see not a single plant that I could identify as having seen before.

I looked up at the hillsides of the valley around me and I felt it almost as an emanation, the sense of something strange.

I ought to go back; I knew it then. I should go back to the cave, to the sphere, and sit in it, wait until it took me home, and think nothing of the shape I would arrive in. For the place was strange and the valley was strange, and even if it was the future, I had no business there.

Then I looked down the valley. I could see what lay ahead of me more clearly now. There were low stone walls enclosing areas by the stream where I believed I had seen the animals grazing, and I believed I could see the roof of a building. It was a low stone farm or croft-house, and must be isolated, for I could see there was no other building for at least a mile.

I should go and look at the animals, I thought. It would be stupid to go back and have to say that I had not even looked at them after having already come so far. And if there were people in the farm, just an isolated family living, a few words with them only could probably tell us everything. I would go and ask, exchange a few sentences with them, and then go back. It seemed simple to me still, and I could see no visible danger whatsoever.

I got up and stood for a moment, and then walked on. There were heather-like plants, I now saw, growing in tufts between the rocks. I could hear a bird singing, and the sound reassured me. I looked for it, being interested in little things.

I saw a bird, the same or another, as I walked on down the stream. It was sitting on the first of the low stone walls that contained and penned the animals, and for a moment I was fascinated by its behavior. It was perched there and peering down intently into a crack among the stones. It was a small brown bird of a kind I could not easily recognize and it had an attitude of bright alertness and quick, fast movements when it fluttered as I approached. I thought at first that it was afraid of me, but it wasn't. It was only that it was excited and eager to get at something that was hiding from it between the stones, and it prodded from time to time into the crack with its bill. Its beak was not long enough, and while I watched as I passed it, it flew down from the wall to the ground and came up again with a dry stalk of the heather. It began to poke in the crack with that and dug out and caught and ate its prey, a long and writhing insect. The action looked perfectly natural and normal. It was only that I felt a kind of wonder about it, such as the question whether our birds had been in the habit of using tools.

I might have thought more about the bird except that now, having reached the first of the walls, I was able to see the animals.

Sheep, I thought, or goats. I looked at them as I walked along by the wall. It was odd not to know which. Some had the wool of sheep and others had the untidy coats of goats. None of them had quite the right shape for either. When I saw one that looked like a miniature milk-cow, complete with horns and udders but about three feet high and with a straggling goat-like coat, I truly began to think.

A dog began to bark at the farm. I had come near to it now, to the windowless, blank side of the low-roofed building, and I was approaching it between the rough stone walls. I had not thought of a dog. I had thought I would go and look before I spoke to anyone. But, picking my way through the mud, I realized that I was committed. Someone was going to come out to see what was causing the barking of the dog. I did not want them to see me back-view, scurrying into the distance. I did not want them to take me for a thief. Even more, I did not want them to follow me.

I had a moment of doubt then, of reason you might say. For the first time I wondered if it were truly a wise thing to appear in an isolated valley, a total stranger in what could only be an outlying frontier district, asking, as an excuse for his presence, about what date it was and what had happened to the world a hundred years ago. But I only thought my mind was fully recovered. I did not see it clearly.

Yet I was right about the effect of the barking of the dog. A woman came around the corner of the house. I call her a woman. I have no other word to use. She was about four feet six, enormously broad, with large bare feet. She was wearing a dark, shapeless garment, and her head had the shape that is usually associated with congenital idiocy. I stopped the moment I saw her. I began to think again, too late. When I first saw her, she was turning, saying something to the dog. Then she turned and saw me.

It isn't easy to explain the feeling as we looked at one another. It was the kind of thing that happens when two animals see one another, strangers, of different breeds. Their hackles begin to rise. It is the sense of something similar but at the same time hopelessly alien.

We solved our problem in different ways, confronting one another across the mud of the farm-yard between the house, the field-pens and the animal sheds. I took a step towards her, trying to look friendly. "I'm sorry to disturb you," I said with what I was realizing even then was enormous futility. "I only want to ask you . . ."

She began to scream.

I understood a little. I understood why Galbraith and the General had told me to stay around the cave. It was only after I had spoken that I even began to think and wonder if

English were the right language. To use it was itself an enormous presumption, presuming that her world was my world, that the two were connected, within a limited time, by history. It was an assumption I was making that I was in "the future," and only now, when it came to the point, did I realize that everything I had seen since I had come out of the cave had seemed to place me in some space and time that was hopelessly, impossibly remote.

Yet it came off, that was the incredible thing. Contrary to all evidence, the words that she screamed back at me were English in a fashion. I could not pretend at that time to understand the significance of it, or the significance of anything else, either.

"Go 'way! Go 'way!" she was screaming at me as though I were her enemy. "We have no childers here!"

I did not pretend to understand the meaning of the word "childers". I only reacted to her attitude. I told her:

"I won't harm you!"

"Go 'way!" she screamed again.

"I only want to talk to you!"

"You moonies!" she screamed. "I'll let the dog! We have no childers!"

"I only want to speak."

"Jeb! Jeb! They're here! A moony's here!"

If it was someone else she was calling to, I thought, she had no need. He would have heard her in the first place. But I was not sorry. It was just fantastically bad luck, I thought, that on making my first contact in the new world I should have found myself confronted by a misshapen, female, dwarf idiot.

I did my best.

"What's a moony?" I said.

It actually stopped her screaming. She stood at the corner of the building with her great bare feet and statuesque ankles, that looked as though they belonged to some figure ten feet tall, planted in the mud, and let her mouth fall open and gaped at me.

"I'm not a moony," I said. I went towards her a little to convince her of the peacefulness of my intentions.

An old man appeared, coming round the other corner of the building.

At a first glance at him I was relieved that he had something like the size and appearance of a normal man. I do not know what I had been thinking. I was to think it again soon, but meanwhile I was relieved. I even thought I could place the situation, the old man and his idiot daughter, the remote farm, and the fact that he looked thin and starved, near dying maybe, but hanging on with a sinewy, active life.

"I'm sorry," I said to him, turning to him. "I only want to ask you . . ."

"He says he's not a moony!" the woman said.

He looked at me with alarm and then with a sly, tense grin.

"He says, 'What is a moony?' " the woman said, and laughed. Even allowing for what she was, it was not a pleasant laugh.

"A grown archaic who isn't a moony," the old man said looking at me with an air of total disbelief.

I heard a sound behind me.

I swung round. I knew it now. I was in a situation that was developing. It was a simple situation but I did not understand it. I did not even understand the language, which was English with wide differences, and I began to have a feeling about the outcome.

And the man who had come round the field walls and animal sheds behind me made it clear to me. I use the word "man" about him as I had used the word "woman" about the woman. It was for want of anything better. And he was advancing from that direction as though he had gone round there deliberately to cut me off.

He had a small, ridiculously tiny head, set on the most massive pair of shoulders I had ever seen. The neck was short and had almost the thickness of the head. But the rest of his body did not conform to those proportions. He stood about seven feet tall, but the barrel of his chest seemed to shrink inwards to the waist. His belt seemed to hold up a pair of ragged trousers precariously above a narrow pelvis, and it was his legs that were hopelessly long and thin. I looked at the bare feet in the mud again. By that time I would not have been surprised to see them six-toed, or webbed like ducks, or ending in bird-like claws. It was just that they were incredibly long and thin.

Don't fight, I told myself. Don't be aggressive. It was contact I wanted, only a few moments of sane, sensible conversation. I had to tell myself that for the way he was advancing on me. I could see it. He had taken one look at me and determined to attack. I just did not believe it.

"Moony?" he said. He said it as though it were an important but somehow dirty word. "You say you ain't no moony?" He had to say it, maybe, to get it into that tiny skull of his.

"He ain't Outlands either," the old man said significantly. They began to close in on me, all three of them. It was just that I could see no reason why they should attack.

His arms were long. When he put them out to me, I could get nowhere near him. I did not want to kick him. I had an idea that I should treat them gently. I was thinking now, at last, too late, of what Galbraith and the General would say if I had to go back and say I had wandered from the cave and done nothing but succeeded in rousing the fury of the inhabitants. I didn't even take it seriously until it was too late.

He held me off, then suddenly dragged me to him in a bear-like hug. We crashed down onto the ground. I had been right in thinking he could be no great danger with such a slender middle. But the woman and the old man ran up, the woman in particular, with a kind of murderous fury. She had grabbed a stake or stone and was holding my neck to throttle me with one great hand while with the other she struck out at my head while I fought with the pin-head creature I could not believe in.

It was the old man to whom I owed my life. "Don't kill him!" he was saying, though he was kicking me occasionally as he was dancing round us. "Don't kill him! If he is what he is, we can sell him to the moonies!"

I was hearing him say that when I went under, knocked out and almost torn apart between the three of them.

X

THEIR LANGUAGE was English. There was a world of significance in that.

There was darkness and an unpleasant smell. I sat up and tried to move and realized I was tied.

I lay there for a moment thinking. My mind seemed at last to have come back to something near its normal. I had made a complete and utter wretched hash of it. Now I was thinking, I could see that. I could not have acted more stupidly from the moment I stepped out from the sphere.

Not merely had I not done all the things I should have done, the detailed log entries, the minute inspection of the cave, the statements every few minutes of just what I had done and what I proposed to do next, but I had accomplished the appalling folly of getting myself captured so that I could not go back personally to report.

Meanwhile the pain from my bruised head and ribs was in competition with a new pain from my wrists and ankles. It was easy to explain. It just indicated the thoroughness with which I had been tied.

I thought for a moment on another tack. The creatures who had captured me. Was I sure? Or were they just figments of my disordered brain? Thinking of them and trying to visualize them as I had seen them, I could not be sure. If they were true, then I had not actually found out anything in my excursion from the sphere, out of the cave and into the new environment. I had only made the problem a thousand times worse.

But it was hard to dismiss them as figments of my mind when I was lying there in what seemed to be an animal shed or garden tool store with a feeling of cold discomfort all around me and light, which must be the last of the daylight, coming in through gaps between the roof and the dry stone walls and under a lower edge that could only be the bottom of a crude wood door.

If they had not been exactly what they seemed to me, they must have been something like it or I would not be there. And I remembered now. One of the jobs I was supposed to do around the sphere was to take star sights in the dusk at this time, and establish the position of Venus if it appeared in the night sky as an evening star so as to date this time and place exactly. I was to do all that just before I settled myself for my return journey in the sphere. And the sight of the fading daylight told me I was going to be too late for it.

In the laboratory they would get back the sphere empty except for the log book with the single log entry and the skull. I did not like to think of that, of Sara being confronted by her own skull as final evidence of the reality of the world that I was in. What would they do about it? Send someone else? Or instruments?

I felt a helpless fury. The pain of my wrists and ankles and of the position in which I was lying had become severe. I began to sqirm and twist from the waist and try to loose my bonds. If the people were of such low calibre as I thought, then they could not have tied me up properly, I thought. I was wrong about that. Even if my pin-headed friend was a mentally deficient farmer, he had learned at some time how to tie up a pig, and it did just as well for a man.

Gasping and struggling, I realized that I could not break my bonds, least of all the cords or thongs that held my wrists, which were tied behind me. But at least I could think now. The mist that had been over my mind since I had made the transfer and suffered in the sphere had at last departed. I struggled and got myself up into a sitting position against the wall. I felt the rough edges of the stone with my hands, feeling each projection I could find with my extended finger tips. I jerked myself along the wall until I found a good one and then, swaying my body forward and up and down, I began to rub the thongs that bound me against the quartzite of the rock.

It would take time. I knew that. I did not know how much time I had. I even had hopes of getting free and out and back to the sphere that night to begin with. It took longer than I thought, and I had to see those hopes fade. I rested a while and then went on again. To get out and free was the main thing. I could no longer see farther ahead than that.

I was almost free and could feel a slight but definite loosening around my wrists when a light showed under the door. I kept suddenly still. I thought it was going past, but it came towards me.

I sat back as I was against the wall. I could only hope that what I had been doing would not be discovered. I listened to a fumbling with the door catch and bars.

The old man came in. He brought light that smoked and seemed to run on oil of mutton fat and a pan of some kind of food. He held up the light and looked at me. "So you ain't dead," he said with satisfaction. He cackled in a way that seemed to me senselessly: "You're like me. You're one of the old type. You're hard to kill."

I did not pay great attention to what he was saying. I was thinking that if he untied my hands to let me feed myself I would throttle him, while if he fed me I would still have a chance of getting free afterwards.

He gloated over me for a while before he began to feed me. "I was like you once," he said. "There ain't many archaics now. How come you're not like Jeb and Molly when you're nearer to their age?"

I had to pay attention. He was telling me things unknowingly. I found it hard to believe, but what he was saying seemed to have a grim significance about the world around me. He put the lamp down and began to feed me by the simple expedient of putting the pan against my mouth and tilting it.

"The moonies want the archaics," he said. "How come the moonies haven't got you before? Maybe you're an archaic who's escaped from the moonies." He laughed. "Jeb's gone to sell you back to them. Jeb would sell me to the moonies except I am too old."

I spluttered at the food and pushed it away with my chin. I licked it off my lips and he looked at me solicitously. There was no harm in him, I thought. And then I thought maybe it was something else. He was thinking of the price they could get for me. He had said they were going to sell me.

"What is a moony?" I said. I had asked that question before, before they captured me. It seemed safer to ask it again than to ask what was an archaic. Besides, I had guessed what an archaic was. It was someone who looked like me.

The word "moony" was what shook me. If anything, and in my desperate state of ignorance, I supposed it implied that the world had been invaded by creatures from the moon. I could even imagine myself telling that to the General if I did get out.

His reaction was to look angry and disgusted. A wretched look came into his eyes. He was disappointed. He had been hoping too much. It was like something at the dead lowest point of human experience. "It could be your head," he muttered, but he was talking to himself, not me. It was only about me, as he held the pan at me again: "It's your memory. They won't buy you if you're like that." He took the pan away.

He could keep the pan so far as I was concerned. I was hungry, but not that badly. "What's a moony?" I said. "You're right, I've lost my memory. What is a moony?"

There may be lower things in life, in a more wretched state, than my conversation with the old man, but if so I have not come across them. The whole fact of being in his world with him, and taking it as representative, that cattle shed or outhouse, had a grim macabre quality. Even to say it was grim was not quite right. It was something worse.

He shook his head over me and began to talk, partly to himself and partly to me in a doleful voice, in an old man's way. He held the pan but did not seem sure whether he was going to give it to me again or not. It looked as though he would rather keep it for himself.

"I knew one once," he said. "Third generation, grand-childer like you. Looked fine too, but had no memory." His eyes became misty. He was looking into the distance. "Right shape, right size. Maybe fifteen years old, this kid was, by the time I knew him. Parents had hid him. Can you believe that. Living in moonity territory, they hid him. They kept him for themselves. They were crazy. These days, who can trust their neighbors?"

He took a taste from the pan himself. He had lost sight of his aim to feed it all to me. He seemed to like it.

"They could have known that by fourteen, fifteen he'd begin to wander around a little,"he said. "Even here, in this valley, on the fringe of the outlands, they couldn't keep him secret. Someone must have give him away. They say Garman, three farms down the valley, got a pasture mower. The moonies came and took him. Parents were punished too. They'd had him all that time, a real archaic so far as anyone could see. So they were punished, and then the moonies didn't keep him. No memory, you see. He wasn't a real archaic. Not a Toolmaker. He only looked it. So they'd lost their farm, but they got him back. Deceiving themselves, I guess. Thinking he, not the farm, was a thing of value."

He ate out of the pan methodically, sitting there in the smoky light in the outhouse. He too was deceiving himself, I thought. He was going to tell someone he had given all that to me. He used his fingers to get the food out, then licked them one by one reflectively.

"They might have known. He was a bit like you," he said. "Not that he couldn't speak. He'd learn the words and then forget them. Learn quick, too. He'd learn to speak in the course of every day. Then the next day he'd forgotten and have to start again. They were glad to have him back. He looked all right. Even behaved well in a kind of way. Then one night he took a knife to his mother. His father had to kill him. Thought his mother was his girl friend. I guess he had forgotten. The sort of thing a mutant kid might do. We've had a lot like that."

He seemed to derive a satisfaction from his macabre story, as much as from the food. He looked at me in a hopeful, puzzled way.

"You try to remember," he said. "You try to look and behave like a real archaic, at least until they've paid for you."

He got up then. He turned to the lamp and took the pan with him. I thought he was going out. But he did not start for the door as I expected. He turned to me.

"Turn over, son. I want to see your wrist-tie."

I had thought I was all right. I had let him go on talking, and then, at the last moment, he remembered to see if I was still well tied. I strained at the thongs around my wrists but I had just not got far enough and they would not break.

"Turn over!" he said and began to kick me. In another moment he was calling "Molly! Molly!"

They tied me up again, and anchored me to a spot where I could do no harm, and left me there all night.

XI

I HAD HAD time to reflect. They told me that the moonies were coming for me in the morning and I wondered if they would have long bodies and heads on stalks and perhaps six legs. They hadn't. But I was only just discovering that the big thing about a quite new environment is that you don't know just how new it is.

I heard voices outside the outhouse, drifting in like the full morning daylight from under the door. They sounded like human voices. They even had an English, or rather American, inflection. It was one of those questions I could not solve. The people seemed to be talking my language in a world that had no connection with my world. Either we were wrong about the time-scale, I thought, and the time was not a hundred years but maybe a few thousand years ahead, perhaps a million, or something far more radical had happened to our world, far more sudden and fundamental, than even we had suspected.

The door opened and a blonde stood framed in the doorway, standing against the sunlight. The climate was like that. Except over the high mountains where clouds drifted they had constant cloudless sunshine.

I checked, looking slowly up at her from the feet. I was taking nothing for granted now. The feet could be normal. They were encased in rough effective leather boots that looked as though they had done plenty of walking, like a foot soldier. I hoped for something of the legs, but they were human, too human, and on the plump side, which was emphasized by the fact that she wore rough and probably homespun trousers. Her hips were of the beamy kind that look worst when encased in hard-boned corsets and best when in the nude. Her sheepskin jacket was open, showing the proportions of a well-developed and not-young female. At least she was human, I thought. Then I recognized that she was more than blonde. She was an albino.

"Have them bring him out!" she said, coming in then backing out again. "We don't want to examine him in there!"

Jeb came in, eager and anxious to please. He began to drag me out and then thought better of it and cut my foot bonds. He prevailed on me to get up, and I managed to stagger, feeling pins and needles through my feet. But I went out, out into the blessed sunshine and open air and swore I would die rather than go into that hole again.

Molly and the old man were standing around too with that same eager look. It might have been an attempt to sell a cow. The girl albino had someone else with her, a man of the same proportions who was equally an albino. They might have been brother and sister, and later I realized they probably were.

Just the fact that they had been summoned and had come seemed to indicate that there was something, however, beyond the valley. Not the whole world was like I had seen it in the valley and the mountains. There had to be a civilization somewhere, of some kind, down in the direciton to which the valley led.

"Are you going to untie my hands as well?" I said. There was nothing like hoping.

They had both spent about twenty seconds examining me narrowly.

"An archaic," the girl said positively, having assured herself at last. It was like a bird-watcher will point definitely and say: "Look, a ring-necked double-quilled ouzel-touzel!"

Her twin brother's view of the situation was more dispassionate than hers. He was wearing a gun in a holster, which gave him an authority of position, and even though it was just an ordinary, and even rather large and therefore out-of-date style of gun by our standards, he had a deliberate restraint and was looking at my clothes.

"He doesn't make much sense," he said.

I kept my mouth shut. I had a feeling that, given that situation in that farmyard I was not going to make much sense whatever I said.

"What is it that he's wearing," the girl said.

I was wearing my sweater, shirt and trousers, and it is unkind to say this, but though most of my garments contained a proportion of artificial man-made fibres, and I had spent the night in them, and in the outhouse, they were still better, in better shape and neater, than anything anyone was wearing round me.

"This could be big trouble," the man said. "Those are

65

genuine antiques. He must have found a source of supply somewhere. He must have dug them up."

He made it sound as though I had committed a crime by acquiring and wearing garments that conspicuously dated from my own civilization. Yet it was what I would have done if I could and if I had been in their position. What I had was conspiuously better than theirs.

I thought about it. It seemed to me that the game was up. He had the gun and my hands were still tied, and there was an uncertain future ahead of me. Sooner or later I was going to have to tell them, or try to tell them, the truth. I was not going to be able to get away with some invented story to explain my presence, because in their environment, and in connection with their unknown civilization, I did not know what story to invent.

"These clothes do come from a different period of history," I said. "Our estimate is that it's a hundred years ago. You are right except for one thing. I didn't dig them up or steal them. I myself come from then."

It was a good try anyway. My statement was received in dead silence.

"An Antiquist!" the girl said.

It was a new word. You know how it is when you learn a language. To begin with I was confused between "An Antiquist" and "archaic".

"An archaic Antiquist!" the man said, and whistled softly.

I saw Jeb looking puzzled and at the same time hopefully avaricious as he watched us. Perhaps he hoped to get paid more for that.

"Where do you say you come from?" the girl said to me.

I pointed generally up the valley, of which we had a good view from the farmyard. I could see the cave from there, but I was not going to point it out to them unless or until my story was accepted and I could see in what attitude it would be received. "I came down from there," I said.

"An Outlander!" the girl said.

"An archaic, Outlander Antiquist!" the man said.

I had only to listen to his tone of voice to know I had got deeper.

He looked at the girl. "We've got to be careful," he said. "Before we know where we are we will find ourselves suspected for having been exposed to contact."

She looked at me and she looked at him. "I suppose we'd better take him in," she said. "I don't think there's anything about that?"

"I will get paid?" Jeb said in a thin, high, eager voice.

"You shut up," the man said. "You'll get paid sometime, if at all."

"I mean it's a three-hour walk," the girl said. "That's a long time to be exposed to contact."

I wondered if they were mad or if I was. With my hands still tied behind me, I stared at each of them and at Jeb and Molly and the old man. "What's this about contact?" I said. "I come from a past time. I know that sounds a tall story. I don't even expect you to believe it right away. I agree you should take me to someone who will believe me, someone with knowledge of the past to whom I can prove it. But this is urgent! I've got to get back to the thing that brought me here. I'm in peril of being marooned here. But don't start talking about the dangers of contact. It's not as though I've been exposed to some disease!"

It was quite a speech, and, considering the position I was in, I said it firmly, in a way that I believed would carry weight.

Considering the man with the gun was an albino, it was impossible to say, but I believe he paled a little.

"You're right," he said to his sister. "He's a bad case. He's carried it to the point when he actually believes he comes from the past, by some kind of self-hypnosis. I'm going to radio them to send a psycho!"

"The helicopter?" she said. "Oh, Dan, be careful!"

"What's it for?" he said. "Except in an emergency?"

"But if we call it out and it isn't needed!"

"You want to be suspected of Antiquism all your life?" he said. And he hurried away, around the corner of one of the walls. He came back with a portable pack they must have brought with them and dumped at the first opportunity. It looked like a walkie-talkie from World War Two. He began to run up an aerial antenna.

As he began to be busy, I began to look at the way out between the walls and down to the stream and up the valley. I still had my hands tied, but I believed I had a chance. There are probably difficulties any time, in any civilization, anywhere, in convincing people that you come from another era, another age. The normal fate of anyone who says it is probably to be locked up as a lunatic or a spy. But in their age, in their society, there were very particular difficulties, as I was beginning by then to gather.

It was not that Dan saw me looking or guessed my intention to make a bolt, hands-tied, up the valley. He thought of something else. He left his bulky and awkward transmitter pack and came and gave the girl his gun.

"Keep him covered," he said. "If he talks to you in any way that seems likely to convince you, shoot him in the head. It'll save a lot of trouble."

"Right," said the girl, pointing the gun at me as he went back. "Now you can tell me the true story and explain yourself. You tell me. You are an Outlander? We badly need some information about the Outlands!"

"Abracadabra-cadee," I said. I could see she had that gun cocked and ready and would be all too calmly ready to fire at me. I was in my right mind now. My intelligence was working one hundred percent. What it told me was that I was sinking ever deeper into a situation that did not make sense and in which I could not win. In that case, I worked it out, I could do worse than feign simple madness.

But Dan was busy working with his radio pack and talking into the built-in microphone. It was all wrong. I had an awful feeling just how much it was all wrong. The radio itself was more than half the trouble. Even in our time all such radios had been transistorized and made much smaller. Then there were their clothes, and the gun the girl was holding. It was not a relic, or I thought it was not. It looked quite new. But the design was that of an old-fashioned revolver of an early date, the kind of thing that required no great intricacy of workmanship or casting.

Even when, an hour later, the helicopter came whirring up the valley, I looked at it with awe. I had never seen a crate that looked quite so patched. It looked a relic. And it all added up to the supposition, which was somewhere in my mind, that the world had not gone forward, but slipped back at least a hundred years.

XII

THANK GOD, I thought. If the conversation was no better, and made no more sense, at least it was more sophisticated now.

We were in the helicopter, flying down the valley, in which I could see the scattered farmsteads. I could see one larger building in the distance, which was where Dan and his sister were going to take me at the end of the three-hour walk. The helicopter was not going there.

"You can talk to me!" he said reassuringly, as reassuringly as a tone can be when it is bawled out in a helicopter. "You can even talk of Antiquism to me! I don't have to shoot you. I have dealt with too many cases. I am immune!"

His name was Liebnitz. I had asked him if that was his father's name, working on the principle that I had once known a Liebnitz. He had looked at me queerly and said stiffly that he had chosen it.

I was in handcuffs and he was a small man with small features and a large head. He was taking no chances. As well as having me secured, he had the helicopter pilot to help to handle me. The helicopter pilot was a normal, straightforward six-foot male, who handled the machine with a kind of fatalistic caution. I did not blame him. I too felt it was liable to die or break apart beneath us at any moment. But Liebnitz treated pilot and helicopter alike with a sublime indifference, the indifference of the large-headed, intellectual and wholly non-mechanical man. In our world he would have been another freak, another kind of misshapen dwarf, but there he had authority, he talked in a way that he at least seemed sure made some kind of sense, and I had to treat him hopefully as though he were some kind of human.

"Can you understand this?" I bellowed back to him above the engine noise. "I don't want to talk to you about Antiquism or any other kind of theory! I don't expect you to believe my story. It isn't the kind of story anyone normally would believe. But why don't you check it? Why assume I came from somewhere else when I can take you and show you and prove to you that the first time I stepped out into your world was from a cave?"

Through the nose of the helicopter I could see beyond the valley now. The hills fell away in barren, sweeping stony hillsides, and beyond them was a plain.

"I sympathize!" he said in his high and intelligent but slightly squeaky voice. "You nomad Outlanders naturally want to keep your resting places a secret. But that doesn't mean you have to invent some fantastic story!"

"I am not an Outlander!" I said. "If I were, don't you think I would invent some story that wasn't quite so fantastic? Do I seem to you like one of those creatures in the place where you found me, who have no intelligence whatsoever?"

In the confined space in the helicopter he put his big head nearer to me to cut down the need for shouting.

"On the contrary, you strike me as very intelligent. We are very pleased to get you. With luck, I hope to make plans to use you. Most Outlanders we get are of the wild kind. We know you exist, of course, you Outlanders of a higher

70

class, but you don't usually come wandering into the juris-diction of the Community!"

"Then why the hell should I!" I stopped. Community, I thought. Moonies! Had someone said "the 'moonity"? Things were at the same time simpler and more complicated than I thought. In the helicopter I was simultaneously trying to build up a picture of the world around me from words and phrases and hints and half-hints, and at the same time argue with a man called Liebnitz who became more ingenious in his mistakenness every minute.

"Listen!" he said. As the helicopter bobbed in an air-pocket, he laid a hand on my manacled arm. "We know you are an Antiquist. Most Outlanders are! Why else should they be Outlanders and either have refused to join or at some time left the Community? But I am a psychologist. You don't have to try to hide these things from me. I know why you tell me this extraordinary story of coming from the past. All slightly mental people do it! They try to hide their real beliefs, but at the same time they reveal them, as though in a parable, another way. I only had to hear you begin to speak and I knew it was your Antiquist sympathies you were revealing to me in this story of coming from the past!"

You can't win, I thought. Least of all can you ever win with a psychologist. Liebnitz was the kind of man who, if you said black's white would say that proved you were insane and if you said white was white would say that proved you were concealing something. They had advanced all right in one way in a hundred years, I thought looking out across the plain ahead. They were even more ingenious than they had been in our time.

The plain was mostly dusty and barren, but there were farms and green patches here and there where the streams from the mountains wandered and meandered into it. I tried to see what was ahead.

"You say you have plans to use me?" I said desperately. "Just what does that entail?" I had reached the point where

I felt that the best I could do would be to get to know the worst.

"Ah!" he said. "You are an archaic, like the pilot here, and that means of course that you will be under the jurisdiction of my friends the biologists." The helicopter lurched, and he had to pause. I did not know if it was an air pocket this time, or if it was just that the pilot was sitting with his ears pinned back and could hear our conversation and did not like the reference to himself. "But I have plans for you too!" Liebnitz went on. "Even as an Outlander, a man of your intelligence is educable. I'm sure you are!"

I could see a distant sheen through the haze across the plain ahead. The sea, I thought! But the sea in the middle of Tennessee? It wasn't. I had the relief of knowing that. I could see the faint, hazy shapes of mountains beyond it. It must be a lake.

"I wonder if I can convince you that I haven't time to wait to be educated?" I said.

"Outlander Antiquism is a natural but only a superficial growth," he said. "It is only ignorance. It does not have the vicious quality of the Antiquist Heresy among the disaffected elements in the city."

We seemed to be talking different languages.

"After all, it is time the Community began to expand," he said with a glance at me. "We are strong enough now to increase the territory we hold around the city. It is a matter of reintroducing civilization across the world. It will be a convenience if you are educable. We don't want to have to kill you all!"

His glance was asking me how I, as an Outlander, reacted to the idea of being ruled by the Community, which I interpreted as being ruled by men like him. I didn't. Not being an Outlander, I had no reaction at all, and besides, I was only attending to him with half my mind. I was trying to make out what it was I could see by the lake ahead.

"It will greatly affect our plans if I can show that you can be educated to become a good and loyal and orthodox member of the community," he said.

"How soon, if I cooperate and become educated, can I get for myself the ordinary freedom of a member of your Community?" I said.

It was, as he said, a city. The ground was greener towards the great patch of silver water that was the lake, and I could see buildings and an urban area spread out in a sprawl by the lake-shore right ahead. There was no doubt about it that that was where we were going, and I was glad it was not farther from the cave. But the lake was vast. I could see now that it was virtually an inland sea. The mountains far beyond it were still hazy ice-topped peaks. They hung in the distance all around the horizon, and there seemed to be no outlet. The lake was fed by the rivers from the mountains, and it must keep pace with their input by evaporation in that rainless area. My God, I thought. The climatic and geographic change was such that it must involve all the world.

"As an archaic, you can expect to be under some surveillance always," Liebnitz told me. "Genetically, as an archaic Outlander, you will naturally be of great interest to our biologists, and, forgive me for saying this, but there is bound to be some doubt about your loyalty: it is to be expected that you will have a hankering for the situation before the Great Catastrophe."

The helicopter was slanting in towards the city.

I felt tension inside me. This was it, I thought. For the first time I had a chance to ask it, of an intelligent man who knew. This was what I had come for. I had the chance to get the information even if, as yet, I could see no way to take it back.

I said: "What was the Great Catastrophe?"

I found Liebnitz staring at me as though I had let him down.

"Don't do that!" he said. "I thought you were going to cooperate and we were going to try to see what we could do together! And what good is that? And who do you expect to fool by those tactics? What good does it do, least of all with me, to pretend to an ignorance that you can't possibly have?"

The only effect of my question was to make him thoroughly disgusted with me as the helicopter came in downwards, slanting towards the city, at which I stared unbelievingly since it was not in the least what I expected.

XIII

As WE CAME DOWN, dropping out of the sky towards the rooftops, the pilot turned to me and said: "We call it Center City!"

They might, I thought. They might have some such name for this noble city of the future. I looked around for the skyscrapers, for the innumerable helicopters hovering in the air, for the magnificent parkways and the buildings laid out in pastel shades. There weren't any.

I was still under difficulties with preconceptions in my mind. Ask anyone what a city or place will be like a hundred years from now and he'll tell you it must be one of two ways, either a magnificence and a store of wonders or a burnt-out crater, a shell of atomic ash.

The actual Center City as I saw it had that force that comes from being in the centre between extremes. I had an idea about the atomic ash business. I had seen enough of the inhabitants of the world by then. The reduced population of the world, the freakish nature of the men who were there, and the variations in the animal and even the vegetable species, to my mind, made the General's thesis the most likely. I was in a post-catastrophe era following an atomic war. I had yet to discover if the hypothesis was tenable.

The only things I could not reconcile with it were the changes in the geography, the climate, and the mountains.

It did not explain the low, stone-faced houses or the horse-drawn transport in the cobbled streets.

Horses? Well, they looked like horses from above as we slanted down to the grass-grown air-strip, that was an air-strip because it had not been built upon but which was otherwise neglected.

The city was one of those places that had grown and not been planned. It had been built by men picking up stones and making houses for themselves wherever they could find a vacant plot of ground. The results were, shall we say, picturesque. There seemed to have been a great variety of men building a great variety of different kinds of houses. I could see a few notable public buildings, maybe hospitals or schools, and one big one away on a headland or hill that placed it in silhouette against the lake. But the rest was an all-too-human muddle of unplanned conflict of ideas and winding streets. And this was the city, without a car, a public service vehicle, or even a railway track in sight, that Liebnitz had just told me was out to restore civilization and conquer the known world, which I took to be the meaning of the Outlands.

"Hold on," said the pilot. "She doesn't manuever very easily when we're near the ground."

He played safe with the ancient helicopter and came down and landed us well away from any of the buildings around the landing strip. Looking out of the helicopter I saw one hangar and one other aircraft there, apparently under repair for it was in pieces. For a community about to go to war, I thought, the city people had the least mechanical sense of any I had met.

It was not just an abstract speculation. Service vehicles were coming out across the strip to meet us, and they were horse-drawn.

I took it in slowly. It was not that I was mentally dumb or stupid. It was just that it took a little time to take it in.

A fuel tanker was coming out to the helicopter. It consisted of a barrel or drum on wheels drawn by a long-haired, big-footed creature I took to be a pony. The driver could have been human. He might also have been an unusually dark-skinned and shrivelled chimpanzee.

Atomic disaster or whatever it had been, I could see they had had difficulties to contend with in getting civilization going again.

A trap was also coming out across the landing strip. I mean a two-wheeled vehicle drawn by what might best be described as a long-legged, high-stepping donkey. It had two men in black uniforms in it. Generally speaking, they belonged to Jeb's type: small round heads over bodies that might have belonged to Greek gods except that an excess of shoulders gave them a disproportion. Intelligence, presumably an intelligence of the calibre of Liebnitz, had been at work, I could see. Given the varieties into which humanity had split up following the genetic effects of atomic disaster or whatever it was, I could not think of a better suitability for police.

The only vehicle that was coming to us the purpose of which I did not wholly understand was a horse-drawn four-wheeled carriage. The creature was almost presentable. It had a vague resemblance to a horse that had not, shall we say, had too many cows in its ancestry. It was driven by a tall, Asiatic-looking, elongated and swan-necked driver. And in the back of the carriage, travelling in some state, and lord of all he surveyed, was another big-headed, pint-sized, slender-bodied dwarf like Liebnitz.

"Doctor Selwyn is coming," Liebnitz said. "Stay where you are for a moment." And he began to get down from the helicopter.

I looked at Liebnitz and the newcomer as he went out to meet the carriage. They were of a type all right. Perhaps, I thought, there were only a limited number of types that humanity could split up into, assuming diversification over a period of a few generations following genetic damage. But Liebnitz had a kind of intriguing, human curvingness, while the newcomer, who had been named to me as Selwyn, had a firmer, harder outline. He might have been blueprinted by Picasso, I thought. Life imitates art. It is the best argument I know for the supression of the artist.

The pilot had turned to me quickly when Liebnitz got out. He kept his voice down.

"Who are you?" he said. "Have you any power where you come from in the Outlands?"

He was talking swiftly and intensely. It was that I think that convinced me that there was life going on and wheels within wheels and that I had better learn as fast as I could about the way things worked in Center City.

"I don't come from the Outlands," I said, eying him cautiously. "The story that I told your big-headed friend is the truth."

"Don't give me that," he said. There was an anxious, almost despairing note in his voice. "We haven't got the time."

I looked at him steadily. He was not going to believe me any more than anyone else was. He was trying to get somewhere, to get something out of me, too. What could I do? I played it for what it was worth:

"Yes," I said. "I am important. I have some power."

It sounded a good, safe thing to say. Human nature could not have changed that much, even in Center City.

"Will you help us?" he said.

He was a normal man, what I knew they now called an archaic.

"How about helping me to get out of these?" I showed him my handcuffed hands.

"We'll help you," he said hurriedly. "Not here. Not now. This isn't the time or place."

Liebnitz had said a few words to the Picasso dwarf in the carriage. He was coming back.

"When is?" I said.

"We'll contact you," he said.

Liebnitz was coming to the helicopter and waving to me to come out to him. The pilot turned away and began to look at the instruments on his panel as though there was something wrong with them or as though he had some urgent work.

"Make it soon," I said to the pilot, and got out of the helicopter. The pilot's back painfully paid no attention to me.

Liebnitz indicated that I should get in the carriage. The police were sitting motionless but watching me with the steady hopeful patience of strong-arm men.

I waved the handcuffs at Liebnitz. I had difficulty in getting down from one vehicle and up into the other. "What's the matter, do you think I'll subert your city?" I said to him. He looked at me narrowly.

The Dr. Selwyn looked at me narrowly too, running his eyes over me with an anatomical and explicit interest. He seemed pleased by what he saw. "We could r·lease him now," he said. "He'll not escape now he's in the city; the women will see to that."

"I'm not so sure," said Liebnitz. "There's been a change in his state of mind."

All the same, as the carriage moved off, with the police following, he took out a key and released my wrists, maybe so they would not have to take me as a prisoner through the streets towards which we were heading through the airfield gate. I promptly looked around for a way to escape. Neither of them could stop me if I leaped from the carriage, I guessed. It was just a matter of finding an alley to duck down to escape from the police. It was true I had been heartened by my talk with the pilot but I was far from placing too much confidence in him. He had too little confidence in himself.

I only understood what Selwyn meant when we began to move out into the streets of the town. It was like a royal progress but productive of the utmost of embarrassment. The first woman we passed was tall and swan-necked, an ethereal vision that had somehow gone oddly wrong. She turned to look, then looked again and waved and began to follow the carriage. She attracted the attention of a matron who was tubby round the middle, who looked and began to follow too. They cut through the traffic and all the other pedestrians, and soon we had a following of females of all shapes and sizes. I wanted to crawl under the seat at that point. I had never attracted such enthusiasm before. I did not like it. It was like being a fertility symbol produced naked and exposed, and there was not one of the growing crowd of women who was natural, normal, or whom I would not have run to get away from.

"Your friend seems to have a peculiar innocence," said Selwyn with a malicious grin aside to Liebnitz. "Can it be that he has been unaware of the role of an archaic in our community?"

XIV

THEY SPOKE TO the driver, who whipped up his horse for a little and succeeded in leaving the growing female crowd. It did not last for long. Another began to collect. The process had to be repeated at intervals. And this was the time I was trying to get a view in detail of Center City.

We were heading down a main thoroughfare so far as I could gather in the general direction of the lake, and I looked around at the low-fronted, stone-built, slate-roofed houses, the variety of vehicles and the even more varied pedestrians who formed the population of the city. We were sitting facing one another in the open carriage, and I said, maybe sharply, to Selwyn,

"What is the role of an archaic in your community?"

I was too worried to stick at describing myself as an archaic.

Liebnitz and Selwyn exchanged those malicious smiles as we made our royal progress. I had a sudden awful feeling. What was their reaction, envy? I wondered about something of which I had not dreamed of thinking before: about just how their kind, with their exceptionally large heads and exceptionally small bodies, would breed. It didn't seem probable or even likely. And as I looked around me at the enormous variety of humanity and post-humanity in the streets of the city, I found my mind was full of questions.

"He is in that state of ignorance?" Selwyn said to Liebnitz.

"I told him he would be in the charge of the the biologists," Liebnitz said to Selwyn.

"All that you were telling me!" I said to Liebnitz. I felt indignant. I looked about me. I felt I might have done better to escape by leaping out of the helicopter. "All that about how you needed me for psychological reasons, as an experiment in education . . ."

"That too," said Liebnitz smoothly. "Dr. Selwyn and I are friends. We work together."

"In what? To what?" I stared at Selwyn. "What do you do?"

As we rolled through the city, Selwyn looked at me with measured pride and satisfaction.

"Naturally, as a human biologist and geneticist in the radiation and post-catastrophe era, I work to find the Line."

He was complacent about it, as though it were something overwhelming and quite obvious.

"The Line? What line? I'm not with you. As I told your friend Liebnitz!"

"Please don't begin on your fantasies again," Liebnitz said. "We know you are an Antiquist with dreams of ancient grandeur. But fortunately, from Selwyn's point of view, it does not affect the genes."

Selwyn raised a slightly languid hand and indicated a building we were passing. Set back a little from the thoroughfare that led through the city towards the lake, it was a school.

I was observing like mad. It was not until I saw the more varied children that I realized that I had been becoming accustomed to the pedestrian sidewalk crowd of adults that filled the city. They were not infinitely variable. If you listed five main types, the albinos, the tall wide-shouldered like Jeb, the squat like Molly, the big-heads like Selwyn and Liebnitz, and the small and chimpanzee-like; then the major remaining differences were between the sexes. The swan-necks like our driver and a proportion of the women could be an F2 cross. I wished I could remember more biology. I wished I could remember the elementary principles of genetics. For a moment I even wished I was not a physics-and engineering-trained rocket man.

For the children were a riot.

They were seething in a playground. We were passing the school at a time when they were indulging in the normally humanly-murderous activities of children turned out to play in a level stretch enclosed by buildings. But they had swan necks and squat middles. They had albino hair combined with large shoulders and/or long legs. They had the bodies of one kind and the threshing limbs of another. And some were like nothing on earth. I even saw one who looked as though he were covered with narrow scales.

"We have not got the Line yet," Selwyn said as we drove past in the carriage. "We never will, uniformly, of course. There are bound to be a number of divergent kinds. But all the same, you must admit that we do better than you do with your unrestricted breeding in the Outlands."

"Better than I do!" I said. For a moment I found it hard to remember that they unshakeably believed me to be an Outlander, a member of another community or way of life of which I could not begin to imagine the details.

"The Line," said Liebnitz, speaking to me patiently as the carriage moved on, telling me things that I, as an Outlander, could not be expected to know too clearly, "is the eventual supra-human stock which must obviously emerge when the period of Discontinuity, the Rift, is over."

More words, I thought hopelessly. How could I understand the period, the place, the situation I was in, the fantastic and full-blown complexity of a civilization, even though they were willing to tell me, when I did not know the words? Driving through that fantastic city I had a sense of disorientation. I was becoming lost.

It did not improve my situation that Selwyn began to speak to me severely. He was a biologist, I had understood. But he chided me. Maybe his science was a religion. At least it produced a morality:

"You are wrong in your wild, unprincipled breeding in the Outlands, whether you believe in it on the grounds of Antiquism or not," he told me coldly. "You don't, I imagine. You just slide into it from your sickening desires and lusts. I don't know if Liebnitz can ever reform you. I would not attempt the thing myself. But our aim is to save a million years of anguish, pain and conflict. You do not know it, you do not understand it, but in nature there is nothing more terrible and cruel than the survival of the fittest. What worse method is there than slow war, starvation, conquest and extermination to find out which is the higher species? Yet a million years of terror is what you will bring into being by your refusal to think, your reaction to the Great Catastrophe, your conduct in the Outlands."

Selwyn spoke coldly and severely, like a schoolteacher on an outing who had cause to reprimand a wayward child, but Liebnitz took him up and seemed momentarily inspired by him.

"It is not only that!" he said, looking at me with an excitement that seemed to come from inside him. "What kind of super-man will the emergent species be when the Rift, the Discontinuity, the period of radiation ends? What do we want him to be? A man like you archaics, a toolmaker with mechanical genius who is skilled in war? Or something still more fiendish and effective? A master of treachery, savagery, heartless and fiendish in all his actions? Those are the survival-virtues! That is what may come out of human selection in its next stage! But we impose on life our will, our purpose. It is time that man took charge of his own destiny and did not leave it in the hands of a God called Nature!"

"To create a creature of peace and beneficence and re-finement," Selwyn said. "That is our object in controlling breeding in this period of change that your people, the archaics, our ancestors, have left us. To see that it is not a worse man who triumphs, but a better man. In fact to create him. To use creative biology, the greatest genius of man, to build him. To bring him into being before the Rift-period of radiation ends. Is that not a good thing? Then why do you fight us and defy us and deny us? It is no more than ignorance and superstition in you, you Outlanders and Antiquists."

They were talking so much, and I was so confused, that I did not realize we were arriving until the carriage rumbled through a guarded gateway into the courtyard of a building. I was sitting with my back to the direction we were going and I only turned in time to get a glimpse of it as we went in.

It was the big building I had seen in the distance at the time when we were landing. It was the one magnificent edifice in the city, in the centre of the city but on higher land and above the lake shore. It was a temple, I thought, or the city's central offices, or the prison, the Bastille of a dictatorial and oppressive government, or perhaps all three.

XV

We emerged onto a mosaic-tiled terrace with buildings with galleries on pillars on three sides around, and I thought I had never seen a place before that so much combined the atmospheres of a palace and a prison.

The inner entrance, through which we passed when we left

the carriage, was also guarded, and then, as we came out onto the terrace, I saw that its fourth side was a parapet above the lake and I sensed the atmosphere of strangeness and luxury.

What was strange was that, after the city we had just passed through, I should find it strange to see that the people, and above all the girls who were sitting on or standing by the parapet and idly talking until they turned on hearing us enter, were normal, healthy young women of my own kind, and what everyone else called "archaics". Until then, I had not seen one normal girl or female of any age, and now there were a dozen at least, with the lake and wheeling white birds as a background, and I could hear other female voices, and some male, on the galleries of the surrounding buildings.

I had stopped as soon as I entered. I had come so far only because we had been closely attended by the guards, but now they had dropped back as though to give the illusion of an area of freedom within what, from the outside, had certainly looked a prison. I said to Selwyn who with Liebnitz had accompanied me purposefully into the palatial interior:

"What is this place?"

"The Eugenics Center of Center City." He looked at me with slight amazement, as though he could not quite get used to the idea that I did not know.

Eugenics Centre? I wondered. The girls had all turned and were looking at me in a certain way, with a distinct and surprised interest. I wondered what I had got myself into. I thought: Oh no! But the more I thought, the more likely it seemed. The guarded palace atmosphere reminded me unmistakeably of a harem, of the women's apartments of a Sultan's palace. My mind began to fill with wild ideas.

"Hold it!" I said. "Just what goes on here?" By stopping I had forced Liebnitz and Selwyn to turn back to me, and now they were looking at me as well as all the girls, and I could see other heads appearing at the rails and walls along the galleries.

"Don't imagine too much," Liebnitz told me with that expression on his face that I had seen when we were coming through the city, of cynicism and envy. "As an Outlander we certainly aren't satisfied with you yet after what must be three or four generations of breeding in the wilds. A severe physical examination will be necessary before you get the run of this place."

The girls, after looking at me, and while still looking at me with their intent and particular interest, had begun to talk and giggle and whisper among themselves.

"The question is, are you a true archaic?" Selwyn said. "You are rare enough even in the city, where we have tried to maintain our primary breeding stock. That you have survived in the old shape in the Outlands is remarkable enough, but that alone doesn't entitle you to breeding here!"

They meant it. I found it appalling. They implied that it was a privilege that they had brought me there. They were looking at me impatiently, as though it were the last thing that they expected, that I should hang back. But hang back from what? I looked at the girls and tried to see what their eyes were saying. I stood where I was, and since the guards had stopped at the inner entrance, I would not move an inch.

"I don't get it!" I said. "Eugenics? Breeding?"

Watching me, the girls laughed.

"He is more ignorant than we thought, as an Outlander," Liebnitz said.

"Archaic children are rare," Selwyn said impatiently, with the air of explaining something that should be wholly obvious to me. "While the radiation of the Rift continues there are variations in every generation. Archaics get fewer. Yet we need them to produce even the primary variations with which we are experimenting. Even Liebnitz and I and our kind need archaics not two generations back in our ancestry if we are to be reproduced. But true archaics! Don't imagine you have a right to this even if our examination shows you are yourself archaic. You must breed true on test to stay here. Otherwise, like our helicopter pilot, you will be out!"

They were threatening me, it seemed, with just that expulsion from the palatial prison that I wanted. But not, apparently if I proved true-breeding. I tried to imagine what they implied. "On test" they said. Did that imply that I would have to wait nine months?

Another thought came into my mind. He had mentioned the helicopter pilot, whom I knew, though Selwyn did not, to be a revolutionary, a dissatisfied member of the community, and probably an Antiquist, an upholder of that heresy or doctrine that I did not understand but which they abhorred. He had said he would contact me, and I had been hoping ultimately that he would help me to escape. But what Selwyn said now cast a light on that. If the pilot was dissatisfied because he had once been in this place and rejected, if that was the kind of grounds on which Antiquism flourished and gained its revolutionary impetus, then I was in a thorough net, in a closed circle, and I could feel the complications closing in stiflingly all around me. I tried to break it.

"Listen!" I said. For a moment I stood in the middle of their terrace with what must have seemed to them to be stupid, bull-like obstinacy, and would not budge. "I've given up trying to convince you, because you won't believe me. But this is the truth! I'm not an archaic, an atavistic throwback to a previous generation as you seem to think. I actually do come from an earlier time! And I don't understand this! I don't understand what has happened to the world, or what its cause was, or what it is. I don't fit into your way of life at all!" I looked at the entrance where the guards were watching me, and then at the parapet, which I could see was high above the lake. I had to escape then, and I knew I had, or I could see myself incarcerated in that building for evermore.

I was scared two ways at once. One was that I did not like their talk of radiation, or a Rift or Discontinuity, or whatever they said it was. It was true I did not understand it, but I had seen its effects all around me in the city. I was scared that every day, every hour I spent in that environment, might affect me in some way so that if I ever did choose, after getting back to my own time, voluntarily to become a father . . . I did not like to think of that.

"What is it?" I said while the girls looked wide-eyed at me, pleased even I thought, though at the same time giggling, to see me create a diversion in what everyone seemed to regard as almost sacred precincts. "What is your world?" I said to Liebnitz who was shaking his head at me. "Are you suffering from the aftermath of an atomic war?"

The other thing I was scared of, of course, was that I would not be affected by the radiation, that since I had been in it such a comparatively short time, they would "prove me true-breeding" as they said and keep me there forever. As what? As a kind of zoo creature on stud? It looked extraordinarily like it.

"I don't think you realize your position, Outlander," Liebnitz told me sharply. He seemed to be taking the attitude that by raising objections and not cooperating with him and Selwyn I had somehow let him down. "When Selwyn speaks of you being rejected here, that does not imply, in your case, that you can be put to flying helicopters or working the electricity supply or doing any of the things rejected archaics can do, in their capacity as ingenious toolmakers, in the shape of useful work. You are an Outlander and so your very survival, as other than an experimental animal, depends on my ability to educate you! And for that, at the very least, I must have your cooperation. Would you prefer to die?"

I thought of fighting then. I had thought already of taking a run and leaping over the parapet. If it had been water immediately below, even after a drop of fifty or sixty feet, I believe I would have done it. But I could see the cliffs beyond the buildings. They seemed to enclose a beach. And even if I survived the drop onto sand or rocks, and could swim out into the lake, I knew that the city stretched away on both sides and I would have to get through it to reach the country I would have to cross to get back to the cave.

It was hopeless, I realized. I could curse myself for not having escaped earlier though I could not think when, but being where I was there was nothing but to set myself to learn, to understand the situation I was in, then to use my knowledge when I had it to engineer my escape by more subtle means.

"All right!" I said, and tried not to show my hopelessness.

"No more fantasies about having come from a past time or Antiquist heresies?" Liebnitz said sharply.

"No!"

"Good," said Selwyn. "Then we can proceed! We will give you a thorough medical examination, and then if you still look like an orthodox archaic, and prove healthy from the blood tests, we will consider using you in a day or two for a trial breeding."

His words produced a sound of excitement from the girls, a titter of laughter that made me for the first time really look at them.

The dozen on the terrace and on or by the parapet were of all ages from sixteen to thirty. They were simply but colorfully dressed, and they had an air about them, a tendency to cling together and exchange secrets as though they were an enclosed and protected sisterhood. Yet they had not been shocked by the talk of breeding. It was the atmosphere of the seraglio, of women so enclosed and sheltered that they saw themselves in a single light and had but a single aim. And yet it struck me that they and I and any others there might be like us, who were prisoners in that building, were the last representatives of humanity as I had known it. We were like creatures in a zoo, last products of an all but extinct and dying species, yet kept obviously as things of value, for breeding purposes, the nature of which Selwyn and Liebnitz had explained to me, but of which they, not we, were masters.

"What room?" said Selwyn to one of the entrance guards. It was the end one on the ground floor, with access directly from the terrace.

XVI

"I BRING the light," she said after she had slipped diffidently into my room.

I looked at her. She was one of the younger but not the youngest girls. She was about nineteen or twenty. She had come in hurriedly and closed the door quickly behind her as though she had had difficulty in getting away from the others and had been anxious that they should not see her enter.

She was carrying no lamp. She was carrying nothing at all in fact except herself and her loose-flowing dress. I looked up at the electric light fitting in the ceiling. Electricity, I had already seen, was one of the few concessions to modernity that Center City made.

"If that is meant to be a cryptic utterance," I said, "you'll have to explain it to me. I'm not yet used to your city ways."

"Oh!" she said. "I thought that even in the Outlands they'd know the greeting of an Antiquist!"

I looked at her again, more sharply now. So this was the terror, the peril, that Selwyn and Liebnitz had been warning me against. It was hard to take it seriously in the form of a slender and pretty girl. I had to tell myself that we in our time were deeply concerned about Communist agents no matter how they looked, but all I succeeded in doing was in making myself wonder if we were right to take Communist agents so seriously either.

"You—are an Antiquist?" I said.

"Not so loudly!" she implored me.

"Come and sit beside me," I said. There was a shortage of wood in Center City. The room had stone couches with upholstery and cushioning.

She came diffidently. "People are liable to misinterpret when two are together on a couch in a place like this," she said. "Besides, you haven't been passed yet."

I thought wildly for a moment of asking her what her attitude would be if I had been. She made it sound as though my being passed would be equivalent to our being married. I decided to by-pass it, my position there being bad enough already. I would meet that situation when the time came.

"We know better," I said. "Tell me all about Antiquism."

She lifted her big blue eyes and looked at me with amazement. "Don't you know?" she said. "I thought all Outlanders were natural Antiquists and you had families and—" She blushed. "That kind of thing."

I could see I was in a position of delicacy. If I were passed as medically fit by Liebnitz and Selwyn then anything went between me and her, but when she talked of families she blushed. I was going to have to walk a tightrope not to appear a moral boor.

"What do I call you?" I said.

"Irimia."

"Listen, Irimia, all that you were talking about, families and all that, seems natural to me. What I don't know is the doctrine of Antiquism and how it affects Selwyn and Liebnitz and the authorities in this city."

She looked at me with big eyes.

"Oh, I don't know that I can tell you that. I was just told to contact you through the channels of our organization, when we heard you were in here."

"Try," I said.

"You know about Selwyn and Liebnitz and their hybrid people?" she said.

"Their what?"

"Hybrids," she said. "We call them hybrids. You know

what they say about using the radiation period of the Rift, and the way all children are different from their parents now, to evolve a new kind of man? It isn't true. They don't want to invent anything new at all. It's only themselves they want to produce, and that's why we archaics are kept here, because we are the first kind from which they are evolved."

I sat quietly looking at her. It might be true. It tied up with what Selwyn himself had told me in one way. But it might be scurrilous gossip. The fact that she innocently believed it made no difference.

"They seemed sincere when they told me they were trying to evolve a new kind of man," I said. I remembered it: "A higher man dedicated to peace and a higher consciousness, or something. It would only be a more savage and warlike man that would be evolved by competition and survival of the fittest in the wild."

She looked amazed that I had believed so much.

"Oh, they are sincere!" she said. "Naturally, they think they are the higher kind of man. All kinds do. That is what Antiquism teaches. The hybrids think they are a higher kind of man because they have an intellectual capacity beyond the rest of us. Only they are—well, hybrids. They have to get over that."

"I only know about flowers being hybrids," I said.

She evidently found it difficult to teach an ignorant Outlander even the most simple facts of life.

"Have you ever seen a hybrid woman?" she said. "A woman like Selwyn and Liebnitz? They are the same. Their bodies . . . and have you ever seen a hybrid baby? Most babies have big heads, but they—it doesn't work."

"How are they born?"

"From two different kinds. From the big squat women and a different kind of men. It's very complicated. It's something to do with recessive genes. And the kind of men they need are only born from us archaics. So they aren't a race, you see, Selwyn and Liebnitz and their kind. They were only produced in the early stages of the Rift by accident, by crossing. They think they're better than all of

91

us, but they can't arrange for their continuance because the kind of men who are their fathers aren't true-breeding either. It's a difficult problem for them. But that's what they mean by evolving a higher kind of man. They will solve it when they find some way of bringing men like themselves into being regularly, by their social breeding laws, and not just by accident, from time to time."

She was looking at me innocently. She hadn't blushed when she told me the anatomical and genetic details, and, complicated as the story was, I did not think she could have invented it.

"So this is Antiquism," I said slowly. "The dreadful crime."

"Oh no!" She looked at me pleadingly and passionately. "Antiquism is much more than that! There's more, much more—I've told it very badly!"

"More?" I looked at her suspiciously. "Such as what?"

"Antiquism is about evolution. It says all creatures must fight against their own successors if they're really new and different."

I stared at her.

"Oh, the hybrids are right about some things!" she said. "It's awful, but what they say about us is true. We are just toolmakers. We're animals that because of what we are have an urge to make and do. Liebnitz will tell you! He'll point out that archaic science—the science our ancestors had when they had a big material civilization—was really just a list of ways of doing things. And it's true! We can't get past it. Look at any of our old scientific text books. All the theorizing, all the deep thinking about what things are, and why, just disappears after a year or two. New things used to be found out that made it nonsense. But the instructions for doing things, oh, experiments and ways of making things, they remained! That was our kind of mind. And that is why we hate the hybrids, who haven't got that kind of mind. They aren't interested in doing and making material things for their own sake. Surely you must see that!"

I did. One view of Center City had taught me that the

hybrids had no mechanical sense at all. Yet I felt dazed,
wondering what the girl was trying to tell me.

"But that doesn't mean you must hate them! That doesn't
mean that they can't make a New Man!"

She stared at me, despairing at what she had to explain.

"It does! Don't you see that if *we* were inventing our own
successors we would not have aimed at anything like the
hybrids! We'd have aimed at a New Man more like us, better able to make and do, because those are *our* aims! Something big and beautiful, like us but more so. But the same
applies to the hybrids! It's a law of nature that they too
must think of the New Man as being like them—because he
would have to be like them to have *their* aims! So they would
never produce any really new creature voluntarily. No living
creature would! Would the reptiles have voluntarily produced the mammals? They would have hated them! So
living creatures can't take the destiny of their species in
their own hands. Nature and evolution have forces in them
that are beyond our understanding. Free breeding and survival of the fittest are the only way. Antiquism sees the need
for the free operation of the laws of nature!"

For an instant, I was not only dazed but dazzled. It was
rightly called Antiquism, this doctrine, I thought. Our eyes
met, and, remembering the basis for our fight for freedom
in the past, I said:

"Irimia! So what you really believe—it isn't as new as
you think, all this—do you believe in God?"

She was looking at me wide-eyed, but her mouth fell
open. She looked pained and lost.

"What is 'God'?" she said.

I stared back at her as we sat on the stone couch in the
precarious quiet of the room. I felt a sense of loss and
anguish. For a moment I had been hoping—for what? For
a meeting of minds across a century? That she would know
what she was doing in restating our old doctrine in her new
form? It was too much to hope.

"All right, Irimia," I said heavily. "What do we do about
it?" I could not say more.

Her expression became pleading again.

"You must help us," she said.

I said slowly, "I must help you?"

"You are a power in the Outlands, aren't you?" She was looking at me with a slight amazement.

It was true I had told the helicopter pilot that. I had done it to give him an interest in me, he and any forces that might help to get me out of the net in which I found myself. And it had worked. The girl would not have been with me now if I had not said that. But I had not expected them—her—to put so much faith in me.

"You are a leader," she said, suddenly looking at me and believing it. "You are a leader of noble savages! And look at you, a true archaic! You are a vindication of our theories. You give us hope our species will survive. And so you must help us! You must help us to bring back to the city in this period of the Rift the freedom you practice in the Outlands! You must help us to seize the city! You must! Otherwise, the hybrids will make their war on you. They will organize their army of the lesser breeds to conquer you. For your own sake—our objects are the same—you must, must help us!"

She was carried away. And were our objects the same? Mine was—and had to be—to get back to my own time. And yet for the immediate move they were.

"Irimia, don't you see? First I must get out of here!" I began to feel a traitor.

"But you—We thought that you would find a way!"

I could only gasp at the extent of their faith.

"Tell me. Has anyone escaped from this Eugenics Center ever? Irimia, do you know how?"

She thought, amazed.

"There was a girl once. She had a lover. A man on the lake. He brought a boat. They escaped, we think. They escaped into the Outlands!"

"Good," I said. "Now tell this to your people. I can't do anything for them while I'm in here. They must get me out. To do that, they must have a boat lying off shore for me

94

here at midnight. It must lie a hundred yards off, darkened, and it must be there at midnight."

"Not tonight!" she said. "You must give them time. And do you think it is easy for us to pass messages in and out of this place?"

"Tonight!" I said firmly, thinking how even that meant that the sphere would have to come to the cave again, and go back empty once more before I could reach it. I could not guess how often they would continue to send it with no result. "And another thing. They must arrange to get me back to the Outlands, not just anywhere, but to the place from which I started."

She did not look hopeful. Perhaps she knew her own organization, I thought. They were much talked about in Center City, but they were about as effective, I thought, and with as much chance of success, as the Communists in the U.S.A.

A bell began to ring somewhere in the building. She got up at once.

"I must go!" she said. "We are to assemble. I will be missed!"

"You will arrange that?"

"I'll get the message out." She looked at me as though I were asking for the moon. "I can't promise. You don't know what difficulties we have. The hybrids are so very clever!" She was almost running to the door.

"Irimia!" I stopped her. She turned to look at me, scared now, for just a moment. Her expression was that of a nun who feared that she was about to be caught in mortal sin.

"Do you want to escape with me tonight?" I said.

"Oh no!" She was shocked by the idea. "It is my duty," she said virtuously. "I must stay here!"

Then she was away, slipping out through my door with a youngly determined expression of sincerity and innocence.

XVII

I WAS NOT to know Liebnitz would tantalize me so much without telling me anything.

I had to know. If there were any prospect of my getting back to my own time at all, it was the drive and purpose of my life to get to know. I went to the window of my room and parted the hangings that had been drawn earlier against the glare of the sunlight from the lake. The sun had moved to the west now and the glare was less. I looked out and wondered how I was going to get out that night. There were no bars across the window, and it opened, but there was a sixty foot drop onto rocks below. Someone had thought that that was sufficient, and I believed that they were right. I looked at the hangings and the covers on the bed, and saw that they were not enough. There was a patch of sand below the building, but that was right below the terrace. I withdrew from the window quickly, hearing steps outside the door.

One of the big-bodied pin-headed men entered. He was bringing food.

"What happened to the world?" I asked him. "What caused the radiation? What is the Rift?"

He put the food down on the stone-topped table. "You eat alone. You are not allowed to mix until your tests are done," he said. He had a high, squeaky voice. He was the kind of guard they would have, I thought, in a place like that. "Stay in your room," he said.

I wondered why they used the words "rift" and "discontinuity" to describe a process of genetic variation and mutation that we had only envisaged as being possible, along with a high incidence of cancer and vast infant mortality, as an outcome of an atomic war. I ate the food and waited.

The man came to take the stoneware plates out. Later, Liebnitz came in. This was it.

He settled himself in one of my chairs and opened a formidable notebook, his small features in his big head frowning as he made a heading and drew a line. "You will thank me sooner or later for the interest I am taking in your case," he said. "when we have made a useful citizen of you and you are allowed a certain amount of freedom."

I walked across the room and turned back to look at him. "Suppose you don't?" I said. "Suppose all you can get out of me is what you can expect from an Outlander and an Antiquist: the maximum amount of non-cooperation?"

He looked at me mildly, and if not benignly at least with a professional lack of antipathy.

"That will make absolutely no difference to your usefulness to us," he said. "It will only disappoint me and prove my methods useless and result in the utmost inconvenience and discomfort for you."

I looked at him grimly. He was too confident and self-satisfied for my purpose. "Have you ever heard the saying you can take a horse to water but you can't make it drink? You have me here for breeding. But suppose I just refuse?"

"We will get over that."

"But how?"

"There are drugs we can use. They are not very good for the mind, but we are not concerned with that. Damage to the mind does not affect the genes. And then there are techniques of artificial insemination. We often have cause to use them."

They would, I thought. I went back to sit on the couch. I watched him writing in his notebook. I could even guess what it was: "Subject antagonistic and non-cooperative."

"Why are you so much against archaics?" I said. "Why do you hate us?"

I had made an impression. He looked up shocked.

"That is nonsense! Are we not doing everything possible, often against your own wishes, to maintain your species?"

"Only to re-create yourselves," I said.

97

He looked at me narrowly. "So you are a sophisticated Antiquist? You know the latest scandal!"

I saw he did not write it in his notebook.

"What is it?" I said. "Envy, because we are true-breeding?"

I was getting through. His face twisted. There was something there. It had been a guess on my part.

"You!" he said. "You with your limited mechanical minds, your materialism, your constant making and destroying. Do you think anyone can envy you when the world would not be in the state it is if it were not for you?"

"We?" I said. I was there. It was the vital information and he was going to give it to me.

"You!" He had an expression of malice now. "You and the wretched, busy, materialist civilization you set up. They were like you, your ancestors. You are just the same today. You want to do something. You don't think why. Endless doing for no objective. Do you know what your ancestors were like? They had an endless transport system that stretched around the globe. And they had no need for it. They had wealth and they had ability and they were living in a vast unexploited country. They above everyone had no need to do anything, no need to get away!"

I wondered if it were his idea of educating me and whether he hoped to win me to him. I said, "What did we do?"

He was as clever as Irimia said. He realized almost instantly that if his aim was to win me he had taken the wrong line with me. But I did not know it.

"But it was not your fault," he said coldly. "We understand that. You were not to know that the specialization that had enabled you to build up your industrial civilization would destroy you. Perhaps no one did. Even we might not have known it if we had not your example. That is why we use no more knowledge than can be contained in one human mind today."

I felt it slipping away again. He had been about to tell me, and then he had not done so. I had thought it would come easily, and instead I had to fight.

"I don't believe you," I said. "Those are abstractions, generalities. If you want to convince me you'll have to prove it and tell me just what happened."

He gave me a knowing grin. "You know well enough," he said. "You know what I mean by specialization. Every man knowing his own work, his own subject, and not that of any others. Trust that everything would work out for the best when your sciences even used different languages! You realize that a man trained in social psychology could not even understand the words in a book of bio-chemstry?"

I kept hammering away. I looked at him scornfully, "What was it then?"

"Worse than that," he said. "And this you probably don't know. Your ancestors were reasonable in that. So long as they trusted the men who were trained in various subjects they had no reason then to know that mistakes could be mad.. They didn't know that a community of isolated specialists is like a man with a split mind. But they aggravated the situation. They had something called Security. It wasn't only that scientists working in different subjects could not criticize one another's work or see how it was beginning to affect their own. They were not allowed to do so. Can you understand that? The insanity of it? Only an archaic mind could conceive of it. They had specialists in Security whose business it was to prevent some scientists knowing what others did."

I had a sinking feeling. It was a distorted picture of our world he was giving me, but it was recognizable. Yet I thought not only of the people and the social system of Center City but the mountain chains, the changes in climate and geography. It was that above all. I had to know how it had come about. I thought I could know.

"And so you say we caused it?"

He looked calmly at me now. I did not know how it affected what he was telling me but he had recovered from the anger into which I had thrown him. He even smiled thinly, as though with pity for my ignorance, to show me maybe how if I listened to him and believed him he could set me on the right track.

"Listen," he said. "Let me give you an example. The state of knowledge as it was in your world a hundred years ago: in the world of your ancestors, when the archaic civilization flourished. The earth is hot inside. You know that? So did your ancestors. They said it had been hot once, like the sun, and was cooling down. That explanation satisfied nine tenths of your population. Why not? It was not their subject. They accepted the simple, facile explanation. It was your people's way. What matter that the earth had been as it was, demonstrably, for a hundred million years? They were busy. They were making things. It was not their business to think how long it would have taken a hot body to cool down in the cold of space. They even knew there were volcanoes. It was an effect of the hotness. It was not their business to wonder why. A plumber was a plumber, not a seismologist. A baker was a baker, not a geophysicist. That was the level of understanding of your population as a whole. A single skill satisfied them. It more than satisfied them. If they knew something about one thing it excused them for inability to think, and crass ignorance in every other branch whatsoever. You had not even curiosity, you archaics, except of a rudimentary kind when children. It was not only that you knew nothing of the world you lived on. The vast majority of you did not even want to know."

Despite myself, I found myself becoming involved in his criticism. I was trying to use him, to turn his efforts to "educate" me into telling me just what I wanted to know. Instead, I found myself wanting to defend my world, to fend off his sharp criticism that he thought was directed against my ancestors, the original archaics, and that to me seemed directed against myself, Sara, Galbraith, the General, and everyone I knew.

"Why not?" I said. "Why shouldn't we archaics have taken that attitude? What was the use of the man in the street knowing in detail about the construction of the world?

He couldn't do anything about it. What use is any knowledge about things you can't affect or alter in any way?"

He looked coldly at me. I do not know if I have mentioned the quality of Liebnitz' eyes. They seemed to look into me and through me and make me shrivel.

"Isn't that it?" he said. "The archaic attitude to knowledge, even in you? Nothing is of use to you unless it enables you to do something. Like a child out of your own lips you condemn yourself."

"What good was it? What good would it have been if they had known everything there was to know about the interior and construction of the earth?"

I thought of those mountain chains even as I asked my questions.

"They were voters?" he said. "You have heard of their governmental system, a democracy? Can you conceive of anything worse, an elite of knowledge without power, and an electorate priding themselves on their stupidity and ignorance? But even those of your people who did know facts about the world knew them separately, in isolation, as separate facts, that, because of the division of the sciences, were never put together! The knowledge was there, you see! It was known, by the geophysicists, that the heat of the earth was engendered by atomic forces. The specialists in earthquakes knew that they were engendered by the heating of radioactive minerals in the lower rocks. The specialists even knew the causes of volcanoes. But there was no one to put all this knowledge together and describe the earth as that nearly living thing, an active atomic pile. And as for the paleontologists and specialists in organic evolution putting their knowledge together, and working with the geologists, to see the whole quite clearly, such things were never done! What good would it do? How many dollars would it have earned? How many ships would it have launched? What enemies would it have conquered?"

He taunted me.

"We had scientific symposims!" I said. "All right! Then tell me: what happened; what did we do?"

His small face looked at me with a bleak intelligence. "You don't know?" he said. "You want to know the details? I must remember that. It is the most crucial thing for a teacher to find out, to discover in his pupil, a specific lack of knowledge that he knows he has. It will do as a peg on which to hang my later lectures to you."

I realized suddenly that he had been playing with me. From the moment I had made him angry and set out to use him he had understood my objectives. He was intelligent. Irimia had been right. He had had no reason to believe that I was trying to discover something, and yet he had sensed it, working solely on what I said. And he had done what he wished to do. He had used my desires to fill my mind with all kinds of useless knowledge that I did not want while he had kept back the main fact. It was with a sense of being hopelessly outwitted by him, of being in greater danger in that Eugenics Center, of mind and soul than I had ever been of body, that I said,

"So you know what I want to know and you aren't going to tell me?"

He smiled and wrote something in his notebook, then closed it and got up and went towards the door. He turned back calmly and looked at me.

"I'll tell you this," he said. "I'll tell you what your people did not understand. They knew, some of them, that the world was, in one sense, an atomic pile. They knew it was a slower-burning source of solar energy than the sun. And others of them knew that life evolving on the earth had progressed not steadily, in a straight-line pattern of evolution, but by leaps and bounds. The cartiligious fish had progressed steadily for half a million years, then suddenly, after a rift in the rocks that could have denoted some kind of volcanic action, their fossils are accompanied by the true-boned fish. A Rift: you understand? A Discontinuity, such as that which obscured the fossil record of just how the fish came out and populated the land as reptiles. A volcanic period, such as marked the great changes in the landscape when the reptiles gave place to mammals. Changes of climate, such as accompanied the ice-ages that marked the appearance of true prehistoric man. And such volcanic periods could only have been caused by special radioactivity within the earth. And evolution, variation and mutation, is caused primarily by radiation that damages or affects the genes in reproducing cells. Now do you understand the answer? Do you know what it was our ancestors did?"

His small and wizened-looking face looked at me mockingly. He knew I could not guess, but he turned towards the door.

XVIII

I STOOD LOOKING out of the window in the moonlit darkness onto the sixty foot drop to the rocks below. I knew I had to go. It was just because Liebnitz knew what I wanted to know now that it was no use my staying.

I could not see a boat out there on the lake in the darkness. But if there were one, or if I could get in touch with the Antiquists outside the Eugenics Center, it would be better to ask them, or anyone, than to let Liebnitz brain-wash me while he tantalized me with my lack of knowledge.

There were so many things I wished to know. I wished I knew how the city, the Community, had started. A place that had been spared, I wondered, in the vast cataclysm that had destroyed the rest of civilization on the earth? Or the people in some survival-shelter, digging themselves out after what they too might have thought was some episode in World War 3, after days or perhaps weeks of effort, to find themselves in a world that had changed around them?

I would like to have heard the history, the slow dawning knowledge, the awareness of the radiation, the realization of what was happening first with the sight of insects and the lower animals, and then the birth of the first human children. What had they done, decided to kill all non-human children? Had the couples who had produced such monsters promptly parted, and remarried or gone to live with someone else of the other sex until it was proved which of them had suffered some genetic damage? There would have been no sure way to tell, except by the event, in a community struggling for survival in a barren, earthquake-ridden and rock-strewn world. Savage mating laws must have been instituted at an early date, of necessity, in a way that cut right across the rights of marriage. Racial envy and racial hatred must have turned to species envy and species hatred as, maybe in a generation or two, new species grew up and their lines crossed and parted. Liebnitz was right in one way. I shuddered to think what must be happening in a state of sheer survival of the fittest, in the Outlands, in the wild.

Yet if I wanted to know any of these things it would be better to ask anyone, even a total stranger, rather than someone in the Eugenics Center now that Liebnitz had satisfied himself about my specific lack of knowledge. I left the window and went to my door and listened. I had already put the light out and left my room in darkness.

The buildings were quiet. Outside, across the terrace and seemingly from above, I could hear faint male and female voices, and a burst of laughter. I tried to imagine what it was like to live always in such a place, with no interest but breeding and genetics and a series of regulated loves to order. Such was the fate of the last of humanity, I thought, the last of humankind. I went back to the window and took down the hanging curtains. It was half an hour to midnight, and I knotted them together and began to strip the bed.

When I had finished, I went to the window and sat silently on the ledge for a little while. I had my improvised rope with me, and I fastened it to my middle. I lowered myself from the window, and with my toes I found a ledge.

It was the way I had decided to get out. It was the only

way. Hanging over the sixty foot drop outside the building I thought for a moment and then began to work my way along the ledge, hands flat against the dark wall, towards the terrace.

There was only one advantage in working towards the terrace parapet outside the building instead of opening my room door and walking to it. It was that this way I would not be seen. But that was vital.

I wished I were in that dim-witted, euphoric happy state I had been in when I had climbed out of the cave and down the cliff. Then, I had been careless of heights. Now my palms were sweating as I pressed them against the wall with the gentlest pressure. If I were forced outwards even a fraction of an inch I would fall over backwards into the drop.

When I had worked along to the parapet of the terrace, I had another thing to do. I dare not emerge around the corner of the building against the sky. The terrace was watched as I had already discovered. I had to take one foot off the ledge, and, with no hand-hold, slowly bend the other leg. With my free toe balancing me by its touch on the wall below, I had to lower my body below the level of the parapet.

The guards were on the other side in the darkness. I had to trust that they would not see my finger tips as I took hold of the lip of the parapet and eased myself along.

I made my rope fast to one of the ornamental pillars that were cut into the wall. I began to lower myself down it. Below me, I could see a lighter area that I hoped was sand.

It had to be. The bottom of my rope left me hanging between twenty and thirty feet above the ground. I could not have gone back if I had tried. I felt that the improvised rope was giving. I let go and fell through the air. Going down, I thought that the one place the parachute landings I had practised were difficult was up against a wall. Only a cat can make a perfectly controlled landing in that situation after a drop of thirty feet.

I lay in the dark shadow under the wall on the sand on which I had landed with a thud. I waited for sounds on the terrace above me. When they did not come, I stretched my limbs.

I was whole. My left ankle was distinctly painful. Only time would tell if it would get better or worse. When I first tried my weight on it, it gave me a stab of pain. I looked out to seawards across the lake.

I could see no boat. I had placed too much reliance on Irimia and the Antiquists.

I went cautiously down towards the water and worked along the beach. My ankle was no more painful than it was to begin with, but I dared not trust it on the rocks. When I came to where the only other way of progress was to climb and attempt to cross or scale a cliff, I took to the water, waded in, and began to swim.

The black water was slightly salt, and cold. It was better for my ankle. I would need it, I thought, for walking later. I swam out to begin with, and then along in the dark shadow of the cliff. The rocks looked smooth and unclimbable and after a hundred yards I began to wonder how far I would have to go to the first landing in the city.

I was weakening, swimming in shoes and clothes, when I heard a soft voice sounding over the water behind me.

"Where do you think you're going, Outlander?"

The bow of a boat slid up beside me with the soft trickling sound of backed oars, cutting off my view across the lake. A hand came down to help me into it.

"It's as well you decided to swim this way," the voice said. "If you'd gone the other, I'd never have been able to find you in the darkness."

XIX

I WAS STREAMING water as I sat in the boat which he allowed to drift in the night on the placid water. He did not say anything at first, just sitting quietly and looking at me as he held his oars as though to see what kind of fish he had caught.

"Who are you?" I said. I thought he would take me somewhere, but he was in no hurry. A boat on the lake was as good a place to talk as any.

"Call me Smith."

His voice was sardonic. It had a different tone from that of the helicopter pilot. It was the voice of a man who contended with difficulties but who believed he knew what he was doing.

"A good name for an archaic," I said.

"You think you could just swim to a landing and walk through the city in wet clothes?" he said.

"I've got to get back to the Outlands."

He took a pull with the oars and let the boat drift again.

"You're a leader of the Antiquists?" I said.

He laughed grimly. "You didn't give us much time."

"Maybe you can tell me something. In the place I've just come from they've been feeding me a lot of stuff about how we archaics are responsible for the state of the world as it is today. You can tell me about it."

"We made our mistakes in the past."

"What did we do?"

"At least we always did things on the grand scale," he said.

I sat quiet. He was not keen to pursue what to him was an academic question. I had made a mistake to mention it.

"So you claim you can deliver the goods," he said.

"Give you support from the Outlands? Maybe."

He leant forward on his oars. "You realize we'll all be killed if things go wrong?" he said. "They don't need us, the males. A lot of us, who produce children of the old normal archaic human pattern are tolerated and given mechanical and engineering jobs around the city. But they don't really need us for that. They don't want us for breeding. They only want the few who produce the particular mutant types they want for their kind. We start a revolt that fails and it won't be toleration; it'll be extermination."

"They need to keep you for one reason. They need to keep the old archaic stock going."

"They have enough of us, the only part they want of us, in laboratory cold storage, to last a generation."

I had heard about artificial insemination techniques. I was afraid that he was right. Even in our time it was common to keep animal semen in cold storage for a year or two and it had been said on good authority that if ever it was necessary to keep human semen for a generation or two, as in the case of atomic war, it could be done.

His voice rose a little, not loudly but becoming harder. "This is survival of the fittest," he said. "This is the last chance of our particular species. Unless we can get our women out, and set up a colony of us to breed normally again, as a species we are doomed. Only survival isn't fought out in the jungle here. It is fought in all the treachery and complexity of city politics. And it is fought on a world scale. Whoever dominates this city now must dominate the earth in a few years time. You Outlanders won't stand a chance."

He let the boat drift in the night. He was waiting for me to speak. I had to think what it was he wanted me to say.

"All right. What is it you want me to do?"

"That's better," he said.

But he gave only one pull to the oars and let the boat drift again.

"You can't expect miracles from me," I said. "You said yourself we Outlanders wouldn't stand a chance." I was

108

troubled because I did not truly know the conditions in the Outlands.

He had spoken of treachery. He had told me, and I believed him, that he was fighting for the survival of what I regarded as the human species. And all I was trying to do with him was to get him to use his organization to deliver me to some point on the fringe of the Outlands from which I could get back to the cave.

He was not a mind-reader. He sat in the darkness resting forward on his oars and he believed I was being honest now.

"You Outlanders," he said. "You fight guerilla warfare. When a column from the city enters your territory, you retreat before it. You've got into the habit of thinking it will withdraw and waiting for it to do that. This time, you can't afford to do it. The city is ready to make a move. It won't be a punitive expedition they'll send against you. The intention will be to occupy, to rule, to govern. And you are going to have to fight a battle against them. You must pin them down."

It was difficult for me, drifting in a boat on the dark lake, bargaining with him about a situation, a people that I did not even know. Before, I had tried to convince everyone that I was not an Outlander. Now I had to keep him thinking I was an Outlander if I hoped to get back to the cave in time at all.

I said, "I don't know that we have the strength to do that. We will lose that battle."

"You must be prepared to lose the battle. You must hold out long enough to get the city to send out its reserves. Then, with the city forces committed outside, we strike from inside and take the city. It's your only hope for survival in the long run."

He waited then. He had put his cards on the table. In the dim light I could barely see him, but I knew there was something about the man who called himself Smith. His was the way men always had worked, with courage and intel-

ligence and determination, for sheer survival. The difference
was that, in a world that had turned alien, he was fighting
for the survival of his species as a whole.

It was my species too, yet I was only concerned to get
him to transport me back to the cave.

"Or haven't you the guts and power to do it?" He said.
"Don't you think you can whip up your miscreant Outlanders to fighting a single battle?"

I took a risk. I wanted to tell him that I was not an Outlander, that all I wanted to do was to get off that lake,
to get back to the cave, to get back to my own time that
was situated comfortably in the past. I could not do that.
Too much in my own time hung on it. I thought of Sara's
skeleton. I had to get back. Yet I tried to tell him that he
should not depend too much on me.

I said, "They aren't all archaics—the Outlanders. You
know what they are. I am a rarity. Why should they die
for you?"

I wondered if I had gone too far, if I had convinced him
that I could be of no use to him. If that happened, I knew,
he would have no further purpose in helping me. A man
in his position could not take risks that in no way helped
his purpose.

"It's still the same," he said. "It won't be the archaics they
will be fighting for, but for their liberty."

He had the answer, but with it he almost offered himself
to me. He was so anxious for what he believed I had to offer
that he made himself clay in my hands, and all his cause.

I only had to say the word to get him to use his organization to smuggle me out of the city and transport me, in
some fashion I could not guess, back across the plain to the
fringe of the Outlands from which I could reach the cave.

I said it.

"Agreed," I said. "I can't promise anything. But I'll do
my best."

He let go of one oar. He put out a hand to take mine in
the darkness. It was a survival, I guessed, of an ancient

custom. I had not seen Selwyn or Liebnitz use it. It must have survived exclusively among archaics. But what it made me feel like when he did it is something I would rather not say.

XX

I LAY IN A crate under a bale of straw in the back of a farm cart. We were jolting and bumping endlessly along a straight and dusty road. By putting my hand through a slit in the crate and parting the straw I got a narrow glimpse of dusty earth, the roadside, and occasional low farm buildings set back and isolated in the plain. Sometimes, when the road passed near a stream, there was a patch of green.

I had been in there for a long time.

I had slept a little. At least we were out of the city. Smith had been as good as his word, hiding me in the cart in a lakeside warehouse before the dawn. Now, all my life, I seemed to have been crossing that plain in a formidable, slow progression.

I tried not to think of Smith.

Irimia. She was another one. She had accepted her life, her fate in the Eugenics Center. Perhaps all the women did, accepting what was common and usual for them in their place and time. Morality was the custom of the community, of the tribe, and morality and tribal customs bore harder on the women than they did on men. But she had not quite accepted it. She had passed messages to and fro and had come to me. Some people might say it was the highest brand of ethics, to obey those customs and social habits that were the will of the community while trying all the same to change them.

We had made a mistake, we archaics, we representatives of the primary human stock that had since expanded into many branches. I still did not know what that mistake was, or how in the midst of our great material civilization we had destroyed our world. I could only hope that we could piece it together, like parts from a puzzle, from what I already knew, if I got back. Yet we had had virtues too, I thought as I lay there in the jolting crate. We were not very logical, perhaps not even very clever, but we had courage and something else, a word we used: humanity.

I turned stiffly and moved my aching limbs on the thin layer of straw that separated me from the slats of the crate in which I lay. I looked out again and saw the same endless scene, the desolation, the rocky and arid dust-bowl which we had made of our world. How? By some means, I now believed, other than atomic war.

Irimia and her kind would perish too. They would live their lives out in the Eugenics Center, producing monsters. Maybe there would even be others who would succeed them, another generation of women living there and a few carefully nutured males. But Smith was right. It was a zoo existence, comparable only with the lives of those all but extinct and exterminated animals that were preserved as curiosities and for possible ultimate scientific use in our own zoos. Once the rest of the species, the men like Smith, and any Outlanders there might be who were still archaics had ceased to exist in the wild, the species as such was doomed. It was like the pterodactyl, like the Brontosaurus. Men, or some man-like creatures in the future, might speculate as to what we were like, and what we thought, and how we lived, but it would be a matter of conjectured history only, and there could never be a come-back.

Yet I had to get back to the cave. I thought about it almost continuously in the crate. I had to get back. I should never have left the cave in the first place. I had been mad, deranged, to disobey my orders. My duty was to my own time, to my country, to the army, to the General.

My country right or wrong, I thought as the front wheel of the cart hit a pot-hole and then the back went into it. It was, it always had been, with us, a matter of allegiance to a country, and never to the species.

Perhaps that was it, I thought in the heat and choking dust that filled the crate. My mind filled with our old slogans, so seemingly irrelevant now in the country and the century through which I was passing as a conspirator, as a spy. My country right or wrong. And: Better dead than Red. Maybe we should have thought more about what that implied and where we would have been if our distant ancestors had always decided to die before they allowed themselves to lose a battle. Suicide pacts were great, but they did not build nations.

Yet no one had told me exactly what we had done. It might have nothing to do with war. And there was that, too. I had seen and discovered more than anyone could possibly have expected, but I was going back without the vital thing.

I went into a kind of coma in the crate. I lay there all that day, in the heat under the bale of straw as the cart maintained its creaking progression across the arid countryside. I did not even know who was driving it. I slept again.

I was roused by the realization that the cart had stopped. Someone was clattering on the box and getting down. The straw began to shift over me. The top of the crate lifted and the face of one of the squat women was looking down.

"Ye c'n get out now," she said. "My farm 's over there. You can stay the night."

I sat up. For a moment I did not know where I was. There were hills ahead nearby in the direction the cart was pointing. From the position of the sun it was after the middle of the afternoon.

I got out. I hardly looked in the direction of the woman's farm. I hardly thanked her. I began to run.

I was at the foot of the valley. I ran along the dusty road for a little way, then left it when I saw a farm ahead. I went toiling up a long dry slope to cut the corner of the valley and avoid the farms. I was running across country, running from cover to cover and avoiding people. When I looked back, I could see the cart still stopped below me and the woman staring. But I had to get back to the cave. I thought of nothing else but that. I had to run across the barren hillsides, and I had only just barely time.

If they had kept to their regular schedule of sending the sphere, it would be there, in the cave, until just after nightfall. At one moment I believed that I could get to the head of the valley and the cave by nightfall, and the next I believed I couldn't. But I had to try. I was not thinking now. All my energies were devoted to forcing my body over that arid waste of countryside.

I could see people sometimes in the fields and farms below me. When I entered the valley, I still kept up the hillside. I hoped they would not see me. If they had, I do not think it would have made any difference. I was getting back to the cave. If I arrived as late as I expected, I would only need a little time there.

Far up the valley, I stopped. I was looking down on Jeb's and Molly's farm. I began to think again then, a little. I thought: my flying suit. I would have to go down to get it. I started down the valley side, coming down to the stream beyond their isolated farm, the last before the valley head. I searched for a short while desperately. I had it in my mind that I needed that flying suit to survive the journey back. Then I found it. I snatched it up and stared off again, heading for the rocks this time, the gulley, and the cave.

I stopped on the ledge outside the cave. I had a precarious stance and I had only a short distance to go to enter the cave itself and see if the sphere was there, but I looked down on the peaceful valley. No one seemed to have seen me, or, if they had, they had not troubled to chase me. I was going to say good-bye to it, I thought. If the sphere was there, in the cave, I knew I would get into it, glad to be back in its familiar reality whatever the transfer back entailed. But why was I stopping then? Why was I reluctant to take that single look into the cave that, if the sphere were there, would make my future actions uncontrollable, make the desire I felt to get back to my own time beyond all bearing?

I found I was turning, still balancing on the narrow ledge.

I began to edge back along it, back towards the gulley.

I was in the gulley again and I looked along it on and upwards. I could see only the ridge of the hill up there, and barren rock.

I went up it, heading for the Outlands.

XXI

I HAD NEVER contemplated entering the Outlands, that mountain country beyond the cave. I went up the slope to the ridge-crest with the expectation of anyone taking a view of unknown land. I reached the crest and crossed it as the sun was setting, and I stood looking out across a wilderness, ridge upon ridge disappearing into the distance, and I was conscious of my own futility.

Where was my allegiance, to my own time that stood in peril, to Sara whose ultimate fate might be working itself out finally as I stood there, or to Smith, Irimia, and those of my own kind to whom I had given a promise when they helped me to escape? The land before me was empty so far as I could see. Beneath the frowning mountains, pink in the evening light, it was torn and folded into ravines and wild gorges. Yet there, if I was to keep my promise, I was to find a people, a wilder, stranger people than any I had met so far. And I needed more knowledge yet, I knew. I knew in part what had happened to our world, but I did not know what single act had caused it. That I should even find the Outlanders seemed unlikely, far less that I should make contact with them, and warn them about the intentions of the city, while that I should get knowledge from them seemed so remote as to be impossible. I could not imagine them telling me what had happened to our world even if they knew.

I went on. I had reached the bare hilltop in the last of the sun's almost level rays while the gorges of the ravaged country before me were folded in deep shadows and I went on into it across barren rocky ground. Below me the ground fell away into the first of many valleys and even as I walked over the crest of the hill and began the unknown and perilous descent, I was starting at the wrong time of day I knew.

I went along a rocky ledge and then climbed down it. I was working down into shadows and the night. And yet I was obsessed by time. As the sun's light left the hilltops, and I found myself on a valley side steeper and wilder than the one I had left, with a stream at the bottom in a gorge-like cleft that flowed in a different direction from the ones that fed the plain, I thought I must go as far as I could that night. At the latest tomorrow, I thought, or rather I hoped quite wildly, I must come back again and reach the cave. I hurried on to cover the most ground I could, and leapt into shadows and took risks in the growing darkness. Yet I was deceiving myself I believed I knew. If I did not cover a great, an almost impossible distance while the light lasted and before darkness finally stopped me, it could take days or even weeks to penetrate that wild and savage country, and I was balanced on a knife-edge between haste and sheer disaster.

How I escaped killing myself that night I do not know. I went down the valley side and along the lip of the gorge, seeking a way to cross it and penetrating deeper into the Outlands at an almost running pace in the last of the light even two hours after sunset. I was behaving as though pursued, and perhaps I was pursued, by a sense of failure, because I had seen so much in Center City, and learned so much and yet not the right things, and only escaped by giving promises I knew I could not keep. And yet I discovered that it was only in men that land was lacking. As I turned a corner of a rock-face, swinging round it on a ledge in a way that would have been fatal for me had it not continued on the other side, it seemed to me that the rocks had come alive. It was a herd of ibex or mountain goat-like creatures that went away from me like shadows, moving ahead and then up a slope that was watered by wind-blown spray from a waterfall and that was uncertain underfoot with tufts of grass-like plants.

I reached my limit shortly after that. Already the strongest light was coming from the stars. I found myself a rough shelter beneath a rock and I was thankful for my flying suit in the icy air. I lay a while and thought.

Suppose I did get back, I thought. Suppose I did not destroy myself in this journey of futility, how would I tell what I had seen to people in my own time? I, and more especially they, had not the words. In my own mind now, I could only tell myself what I had seen and known by using words like "archaic" and "Antiquist" and "hybrid". To tell them anything, I would have to teach them a language to begin with.

I lay there looking out from my rock, that formed a shelter and shadow over me, across the valley at the farther valley side, at a part that I had not seen in daylight, and at the mountain crags and slopes and hilltops that I could see faintly as a darkness against the sky beyond. And I was like the chief of some savage tribe, I thought, that had been transported by air for political reasons and shown the wonders of New York. "Go back and tell your people what you have seen," they might say to him. But I knew now how futile that was. He would be talking a foreign language if he tried to tell them. It would be pointless for him to talk of the wonders of the buildings and the city transport system when they could not envisage a city in the first place and had no words for "train" or "bus".

It was deeper than that, I thought, looking at those black crags against the stars. Lacking the words, they would not even have the concepts.

And then a light shone out.

I want to be clear about it. It seemed to me to be a light.

117

It was like a searchlight revolving, or a far-away light-house beam rotating, on an infinitely distant crag, and I thought at the time that could not be. I was in a land that was said to be populated by the wildest savages.

The light was there to my eyes and senses. It flicked on and off in the spaces of the darkness, a fixed point in the infinite solitude of open country. And, strangely, it seemed to affect my mind and fill my soul with longing.

It was my imagination probably, I thought, that the light, having revolved and swept the country, came back and settled itself, for a few seconds duration of a steady beam. It seemed it shone on me.

It was gone, and the night was as dark and empty as before. A camp-fire, I thought, of some distant nomadic people. I knew there were some people somewhere.

I tried to persuade myself that the light had had the flickering form of firelight. I lay looking out into the night for a long time before I fell asleep.

I was awake an hour before dawn and cold and hungry, believing nothing except that I should get back to the cave and go back and tell my story. I remembered the light in the night and looked at the distant crags. I could see nothing there. I felt in the pockets of my flying suit and found an emergency pack, a flat can of food, enough for a single meal. That settled it, I thought. I ate the food but had to wait until later, until I crossed a stream, to get a drink. I would go on, not in a wild rush but steadily, until an hour before noon. Then I would have to begin my journey back.

I went on, and nothing happened. The stream in the gorge, I discovered, sank ever deeper into a rocky cleft that became virtually a tunnel, and when I came to a rocky bridge where a slab from a land-fall had fallen across the gorge, I crossed it. I sought the high ground again then, attempting to follow a ridge that led in what was generally the right direction, keeping my back to the cave and running deeper into the Outlands.

It was at this time that I began to be troubled by visions. They were not credible visions. At least at first there seemed to be no deception in them. Naturally their first effect on me was to make me worry about my state of mind. When I saw what seemed to have the form and shape of an old Germanic warrior standing on a rocky outcrop about a quarter of a mile away, and when I looked again he vanished, I thought of the strain I had undergone, the strangeness, and I wondered what happened to people who were in a totally alien environment for a long time.

I went on. It was not yet mid-morning. I reacted in the way people do when they first feel themselves troubled by halucinations. I refused to accept that I had seen anything at all. While I might have taken it that it was a sign I should go back, I became a shade more obstinate. I was all right, I felt. I was even feeling quite well by then, and I refused to believe in visions in country of inspiring grandeur, where I was walking and making tiny, even trivial progress under the shadow of great white peaks that hung in the sky to my left, in clear mountain air. It was certainly not going to make much difference. I would go on till noon.

I turned and surveyed the country from my ridge. I had a feeling then as though someone was reaching for my mind. I resisted it strongly as people do a stranger's deliberate touch. And then I realized I could see a tiny trail of human beings crossing a distant hill slope.

Humans? They could be. The leader, seen from that distance, seemed to be a generously proportioned, hairy man in furs. He was followed by two or three smaller and more slender figures similarly dressed, one of whom seemed to be carrying something in her arms. Behind them was a straggle of youths and children.

They fitted my preconceptions, the ideas I had acquired about the Outlands. But I took my eyes off them for a moment and they were gone.

Not only were they gone, but assuming that the hillslope was where I now saw it was, I could not have seen them as I had in the first place. They would have been far too small and distant. They must have been enlarged. They were another vision.

I felt the reaching for my mind again, a sensation that was soft and quite insistent. Dimly, I seemed to hear a voice. It said: "Who are you and what are you? You are not the right kind. You should go back."

I do not believe in telepathy. It is one of those airy nothings that people like to believe in as a fancy. The way the events impressed me was that in broad daylight, in dangerous mountain country, I was hearing voices and seeing visions.

I stood where I was on a flat shelf of rock, on the ridge with a valley and mountain crags beyond, and thought: I am not mad; I am a hard-headed materialist archaic; I was even chosen, long ago at the rocket base, for my equilibrium of character; and I have every intention of going on at least till noon.

"Thank you," the voice said. "I see your mind unclearly, but you must go back."

It had answered my thoughts. I went forward. I had not come all this way for nothing. I found myself confronting a machine-gun post, two men in a fox hole with a gun trained in my direction, a hundred yards ahead. I went towards it. The movement was automatic. I had come to make contact and that was what I intended to do. I had even begun to raise my hands. It disappeared.

"You must go back!" the voice said firmly. I believed I detected in it a note of annoyance. It was searching in my mind for more visions. It was from my own mind these visions came. I knew its weakness. It could only show me what I already had.

"Show yourself!" I said. I did not need to say the words. The thought was enough, but I looked around from that high ridge and there was no one there. The ground was a series of steps and rocks along the ridge. I went along them towards the mountain, towards the valley at the other side. "You can't stop me," I said.

"I will."

"But how?"

"I will show you another vision."

I laughed grimly. If visions of a machine-gun post, of

stone-age man and a Germanic warrior did not stop me, I could not see that anything else would. I was going to make him show himself. I was under the impression that he was there.

I stepped from rock to rock. Some of the gaps were big. I was in the air, stepping out for a rock, when I saw it was not there. The rock towards which I had launched myself had vanished.

I fell heavily on rocky ground, twisting my ankle and striking my head against a stone. I must have been unconscious for a little time.

It was the same ankle, the one I had damaged when escaping from Center City.

XXII

I HAD KNOWN, even as I fell, that I was going to be in a desperate situation if I injured myself while alone, so far from the cave, and in an exposed position in the Outland mountains.

I knew it was gone, my hope that alone and unaided I would get back to the cave that night. I did not know if I would ever get back over all that land that I had crossed. The sphere, the laboratory and Galbraith and Sara had never seemed so far away.

What I heard was voices.

"An archaic moony. There were some items of his private experience I did not get, but he described himself as an archaic."

"How clear have you got him? Is he in good range of the transmitter now? Can you scan him clearly?"

"He's on the line-of-sight beam. I should have the pattern complete, when he comes alive, inside two minutes."

I wondered where I was. I was sprawled on the ground. The view before my eyes, when I opened them, was a chain of mountains, white peaks and a volcano among them, leaning over at an impossible angle. I adjusted my idea of the horizon and discovered which way was up. I began to struggle.

"Heron? This is Widgeon here. He's got some memory of rocket firing. I don't get this pattern. Moonshot rockets aren't in the technology of the city, are they?"

"You must b mistakcn, Widgeon. The only people remotely dreaming of that technology today are those on the Atlantic continent. We ~urselves won't touch it. It's too expensive."

"What about China? He doesn't seem Chinese. But these memories are quite clear. I'm getting constant pictures of big machines. There's even something about a synchrotron. Where's Teal? Teal, I'm calling you in the Yang-Tse islands. This is Widgeon, California."

"Hello, Widgeon. I am working Seagull, France. Is this important?"

"Subject here, Teal, shows images of rocket firing and something called a synchrotron. How advanced recently is the Tibetan pocket of technology? I'm trying to trace him."

A female voice cut in:

"Widgeon and Teal. This is Seagull, France. Widgeon is making Class Two mistake I think. He's confusing live memories with reading, fiction. I know, I did it recently."

I sat up. It was natural to hear voices and singing sounds after a blow on the head, I thought. I looked at the mountains, the desolate scene around me. How was I going to get back? I tried to get up and pain shot up my leg. I collapsed back to the ground again and crouched and held my ankle.

"With all due respects, Seagull, I don't make mistakes like that."

"Widgeon, this is Heron. In this world, such memories are impossible."

"You suggesting he dropped from the sky, from Mars? His most recent memories are of the city."

I sat quite still. The voices were clear and loud now. They faded when I bent to hold my ankle and put my head behind a rock. I lifted my head and looked over the rock. High on a crag on a mountain across the valley I could see what looked like an automatic radio transmitter that I had not picked out before. For a moment I thought it was another vision. Then I saw that that would be the place, and the height, from which I believed I had seen the light, the rotating beam, the night before.

"Widgeon? This is Teal. Did you say a synchrotron? This is interesting. I suggest you hook him into circuit."

Transmitter, I thought! I wondered if it were possible. The tiny electric currents, the cellular circuits of the brain. But we, with our most sensitive instruments, had only been able to record the most general wave-patters of electrical energy in the brain.

"He's in. I'm not sure he knows it."

I looked down into the valley. There was nothing there. Some patches of green and a stunted bush or two in the valley bottom. I was in wild and desolate country. I was going to have enormous difficulty getting back. I could feel the state of my ankle now. It was possible that I was delirious. I decided to treat the voices as real.

"I know I'm in," I said. "Who are you? I've come here to bring Outlanders a message from the city."

I was met with a response of silence through which I could feel at least half a dozen people, scattered round the world, just listening to my mental voice. I do not know how I knew it. I just did. As soon as I threw myself into the contact I seemed to be aware, simultaneously, of a million things, of a scene through a window onto a wooded tree-slope, of a half-barren, crop-bearing island in the middle of a yellow flood, of a rocky, cliff-top eerie above a raging sea. And there was something more than that, an elusive quality. I was in contact, I knew instantly, with a different type of

123

mind. It was a kind that persisted through all the individuals. It was not like mine.

I had a sense of a crowd of individuals pressing up to look and then withdrawing. I knew what it was. I could feel it as their withdrawal-reaction. If they were alien to me, I was even more alien to them. It was a sensation we might have if we had tentatively offered intimate contact to a chimpanzee and found he took it and pressed his face against us.

It left me disillusioned.

"What is this message you say you were bringing to the Outlanders from the city?" The voice came to me formally and seemingly from far away.

I wished I could see them. It was that more than anything that I lacked. They were beings, creatures I imagined of warmth and light. I had, for an instant, been allowed close contact with them. During that period I had even been able to see out through their eyes and sense their quality of mind. But none of them, I guessed, had been looking in a mirror. And now once again, and from then on, I was only hearing voices. I wished I had known that moment was coming, and what it meant, so that I could have taken greater advantage of it when it came.

I cannot explain this. As I have said, it is partly that I do not have the words and partly that I do not even have the mental concepts to tell what I saw and felt. It was what Irimia had told me. I had a sense of only a dozen or so of them, rare creatures, scattered around the world. I was conscious of their difference from myself. But it was the nature of that difference that set up in me a hopeless longing. Their whole aim, the nature of their lives was different as Irimia had told me it would be and must be in quite new creatures.

And I, by their withdrawal, by their use of formal words, was rendered lonely. I had a sense of their eyes looking at me while I could not see back. I was alone again on a silent summit, and I knew they could see me there while I could not see them.

I was a lone creature, injured, with a damaged ankle and far from my base, my lair, and I knew they would have sympathy with me, as we would with any injured animal, except that there was something else for them, some other, larger plan, the nature of which I tried to, but could not, grasp.

"The city is about to invade the Outlands," I said. I was met with a silence, not words but a sense that they knew that already. "I was to organize the wild Outlands tribes to resist," I said. "I cannot do it. It is a matter of the survival of the archaics within the city."

I was throwing myself on their mercy as I confessed. It was all I could do. They were not the Outlanders I had 'ome to find. They were at once far fewer, and farther away, and infinitely greater.

Their words came to me clearly, but cooly and without expression as they communicated with one another.

"You having trouble with the American City, Widgeon?"

"Not greatly. It is at present ruled by the hybrids who are an evolutionary *cul-de-sac*. That must be altered."

"You will not intervene on behalf of the archaics, surely?"

"Not exactly. They are an impossible political influence. Their descendents have not mastered it any more than their ancestors did. There is a swan-necked variety there that has the virtue at least of tolerance."

So much for Smith and Irimia, I suddenly thought and realized. They would make their revolution and someone else would claim it. I did not know how the Voices would manage it, I thought bitterly, resting on one knee with my hand on a rock like a man communing with himself on my lonely summit. But they would do it. Few of them there might be, but I had a sense of power, of certainty, of unknown aims to be accomplished in every inflection of their voices.

Then I felt them turn their attention to me again, not malevolently but insistently. That was one of the ways in which they differed from us, their lack of indifference. I was something they did not understand, and *therefore* they had to know.

"Who are you?" This time it was a silent question from many voices.

I attempted defiance. "Who are you?" I said.

They began to take me apart. I could feel them stealing, quite irresistably, across my memories. It was like a process of dissection, but mental, like knives and deep dredges entering my mind and bringing up my most trivial memories to the surface, even memories I did not know I had and things I believed I had forgotten. I did not know if I would survive the process, and if I did I knew I would be a changed man, as people are said to be after total psycho-analysis.

"Stop!" I cried.

They stopped. They did not wish to harm me. It was only what they had to do in pursuance of some plan that was greater than anything I could think of. And if I cooperated, I felt, as though a warm current were flowing round my mind, healing their incisions, there was no need of it.

"We are the seed," the female voice of Seagull told me gently. "The survivors and progenitors. Our children are the new beginning, the inheritors from the Rift."

She told me knowing that I would not understand it, as an adult will reason with a child.

"I have come out of time," I said.

I expected at least some surprise, but there was none.

"That," Heron said quietly, "is exactly what we were afraid of."

"Tell me," I said desperately. I could not see them. I fixed my gaze on the distant mountains. "What was it, this Rift? I must find out. That is what I am here to do! I must find out what caused it."

Their voices talked among themselves then. They did not address themselves to me.

"He knows too much already," Teal said, that voice that, if I was to believe them, was in far-off China.

"It is a question of whether I can let him go back," said Widgeon. "What can I do with him?"

"We do not kill," said Seagull.

"It may be necessary," said Heron, "to maroon him somewhere."

I cried out to them, actually speaking the words out loud, I believe, so that they echoed over the silent mountains: "I don't know, but I must know! It is a question of the survival of our world!"

They were silent, apparently in some kind of contemplation.

"I propose to let him go back," said Widgeon.

The silence took on a tone of gravity and dissent.

"He is a small thing," said Widgeon finally, having noted their feeling but going against it. "Though he has tampered with time, I do not think he has the strength and intelligence to do us any harm."

He addressed himself to me.

"You will go back," he said. "You will go straight back, at once. And you will not attempt to come this way again. You will find out nothing."

I looked at the rocks around me. I moved my ankle and winced with pain. He "saw" my thought.

"Sit down," he said.

I sat down.

"Now take your foot in one hand and your leg in the other. Let me direct you!" He sounded near.

I felt that someone was reaching into my hands. He was putting on my hands and arms like a pair of gloves. I relaxed and tried to let him treat me as a doctor. My own hands gripped my leg and foot. I had a moment of excruciating pain as he pulled and twisted. It was incredible that I could bear to do it. But it was he who had control of the motor nerves of my arms and hands, not me. I felt him withdraw like an actual body moving away from just behind me then flicking into the distance.

"It is finished," his voice told me. It sounded away in circuit again, no doubt from California.

"How do you do it?" I said. I stood up on my leg again. It felt stiff and it hurt, but it worked. "Thank you."

"It is the particular tendency of our development that has enabled us to specialize in neural-electrical techniques and electrical propogation," he said. He spoke with perfunctory cheerfulness. "It is the ultimate power."

I turned and began to walk down the hill and the mountainside, back the way I had come. It was pointless to argue with him or any of them. I knew that now.

The sun had moved to the west. I knew I was not going to get back that day.

XXIII

I THOUGHT about it as I camped under the rock again that night, arriving to a foodless camp after a limping progress.

What was it? What had I heard and seen and done? I had fallen, and struck my head against a rock and twisted my ankle. I had been light-headed.

I lay there watching the last of the light fade from the peaks and the shadows creep up the valley and the darkness deepen to the sound of falling water from the gorge. I watched, looking away over the valley at the distant crag.

Irimia had said no creature could contemplate its own successor. Liebnitz had said that for man, his kind of man, to control and guide evolution, would be the only way of avoiding strife and bloodshed and the cruelty of survival of the fittest for a million years. But both of them were theorizing. Neither had been to see, as a true scientist would, what was actually happening in the Outlands.

I had been into the Outlands. I was still in them, against

128

my will. And I must not sleep, I thought. I must wait to see if that beam shone out again, as it had the previous night. I must find out if what I had seen, or rather what I had heard and felt, was real.

How had they set up that transmitter, if it was one? How had they done anything, a dozen creatures, separated and isolated around the world? But then how had man ever done anything, *homo sapiens*, our own species, born incredibly in Central Asia in an ice age?

I must not sleep, I thought.

Man had had one great gift, his use of tools. But that was past now, in this age and time. I had seen a bird use a tool, I remembered, when I had first come into the new environment. Tool-using, tool-making even, was no longer man's unique possession, and the birds, many species of them, were even later in the evolutionary chain than man. They were ready, they were waiting to take over if anything happened to man and his many descendents of human kind.

But the people who called themselves the Seed, I thought, had no need actually to come to the place to set up that transmitter. It must be within range of another transmitter, be one of a chain. And if they wanted anything done they had only to take over some other creature, as Widgeon had taken over my arms and hands as he had set my ankle. Any creature would do for them, provided it had a brain and hands. I understood what he meant when he calmly said they had the ultimate power.

A new kind of tool. A new kind of ability. But not only that. A new kind of experience too. I had been granted, if only for an instant, an entry into their communion. It was sad, I thought, that I had not known what pure intimacy and understanding was before. I had not realized that we humans, we *homo sapiens*, were limited; that we were not the best kind that could ever be. And I did not find it any easy knowledge.

Our communications systems, proud as we were of them, were infinitely laborious by comparison. We could span the world with words, we said. And so we could, with the aid of a vocabulary that it took us a third of a lifetime to acquire, with the aid of a giant industry devoted to turning those inadequate symbols for our ideas into electro-magnetic waves, then turning them back again into sounds, so that air waves reached the ears of a listener and resulted, all too often, in misunderstanding.

The Seed, the Voices, communicated directly, by electrical impulses, from mind to mind. I had heard them as words, true, but they could communicate as well by images. Their memory store was held in common. They knew, they did not interpret, one another's feeling. Speech had been man's greatest and most useful tool, but they had far outstripped it. They were living in a quite new sphere of experience and existence, and because of that alone they were man' successors.

Lying there, watching the stars move slowly overhead, I found myself looking out at the sky as into the depths of the universe. Irimia had not known what she was saying, I thought, when she had asked me "What is God?" Dull earth had taken life upon itself and they become humble crawling creatures. In a flash of time, as eternity went, they became beings who looked to the universe as a whole and thought of it with wonder as they tried to comprehend it, and who sought to claim it. Maybe we, man, never would claim it now, I thought. But life would. Life moved like a growing blaze across and through those electro-magnetic fields that were the endless evolutions of the stars. Through a universe of space and matter that science, as it comprehended it, made steadily more abstract, life moved as an expression of will and power and purpose. And we, dull humanity, had never understood but only wondered about our aims.

We flickered into consciousness here and there, tiny eyes and minds and mouths in the stream of life. We came, and opened our eyes in wonder, and we went. This life of ours seemed puny, useless, so full was it of questions that remained unanswered. Yet each eye was brighter, each mind was larger, clearer, more comprehensive. With each new being, poet, scientist or musician, a world was born. What

"Judgen. Take these on your tongue. Keep them in your mouth and bite them when the transfer starts." Drugs. They had gotten my report about the outward journey. That was why I had been unconscious.

I tried to sit up. I knew where I was now. I was back in the laboratory, on the safe side, after being taken unconscious from the sphere. As I moved my head I saw a doctor standing over me with a hypodermic needle, Sara standing beside him with an expression of care and anxiety on a harrowed face, Strassen stripping off a protective suit, and Galbraith and three people I did not know with the General in the background.

"Howard!" Sara said. "Lie still! Don't spoil it now. If you knew how we've waited for you these last two weeks!"

Two weeks. It did not register in my mind at first. I was lying back again, thinking how well they had prepared for my return, a doctor and specialists in attendance, and even a couch for me to lie on and Strassen ready to go in and get me from the sphere. And then I thought: two weeks!

I sat up abruptly. I said: "Two weeks?" I stared at them, no longer mentally hazy now. Their drugs, whatever they were, had saved me from that. But I began to work it out: the day I left, the day in Center City, the day of my escape—it was nothing like two weeks!

"Take it easy, Judgen," Galbraith said. "Time doesn't run at the same rate at the place you've been to as it does back here. Waiting, we've found that out!"

Sara had come to me. She was standing by the couch on which I had been lying. Her hand was on me and her arm around my shoulders, trying to ease me back. "Wait, Howard, wait!" she was saying. But I put my arm around her waist and dropped my feet off the couch. I sat up and faced them.

"But you don't know!" I said.

"No," said Strassen, taking his foot out of the leg of the silver-coated protective suit. "We don't know where you've been or what you've been doing since the sphere came back empty except for the log book with that inexplicable, crazy message of yours!"

I simply sat there staring at them.

Galbraith, looking queerly at me, said: "It's been particularly hard on Sara."

I took her hand. I was sure it had. Sending the sphere repeatedly and having it come back empty. Sending it—but there just had not been that number of days over there for it to appear. I was back all right. We were faced with a major discrepancy in all our thoughts and theories.

They were looking at me expectantly. The doctor leaned over me and pulled back my eyelid and looked at the pupil. "He's all right," he said. "He'd better not move or try to go anywhere yet a while, but he can talk." And I sat silent knowing that I had better be careful just what I said.

The General had been patient. His expression was savage. He knew as well as I did that there had been things we had not expected. The effects of the transfer on me had not been something I could help and he was not suggesting yet that I be courtmartialled for a breach of orders. But he was waiting with increasing urgency for an explanation.

"All right, Major! You can talk!"

"Yes, Sir. There's a whole world over there. I've a long report to make. This isn't going to be a matter of a few words."

Strassen freed himself from the suit. He came over and looked down at me, wondering, conscious. Galbraith's eyes had narrowed.

Reckman, whom I had not noticed somewhere in the background, was indefatigably pursuing the security angle. He was saying formally and insistently, "Will all civilians and personnel not actively engaged in the experiment please leave the room!"

I watched them going, the doctor taking a last look at me, not hiding his annoyance that he had been called in, kept waiting maybe a dozen times for nothing, and now, when things were interesting, he was being dismissed. But it was a closer, and at the same time harder and more knowledgeable gathering that was left behind in the now all-too-familiar underground laboratory.

"It's something Strassen said just now," I said.

They looked at Strassen, except Sara who looked at me and then the General. "Does he have to talk and think just now?" she said.

I was all right, I believed. I squeezed her hand. "How long have you been sitting at the control desk?" I asked her. Then I looked at Strassen. "You got my message," I said. "The log book. You got them when the sphere came back without me on the first day?"

They were all watching me. They did not know what it was about, but they were watching. Strassen looked at me and then went across the floor of the laboratory and round the control desk. He went to the book shelf where they kept technical notes and data in bulky files. He came back with my original log-book, the one I recognized as empty but for a single entry. He showed it to me and I read what I had written again, the entry in the middle of the page scrawled in what looked like a child's handwriting that I could hardly recognize as mine.

I read it out to them, first saying:

"You say the sphere was empty apart from this?"

"Yes," said Strassen.

"I am sending you the skull," I read. "I cannot come back at once. This journey is very bad. If you send someone else, put him in an iron lung and give him sedatives before you send him."

I looked at them all, first at the General and then specifically at Galbraith.

"What happened to the skull?" I said.

They looked as though they did not understand me, or did not believe me. I could have been introducing something for their confusion.

"You mean you sent it?" Strassen said.

"I sent it," I said. "I put the log-book in the sphere and the skull on top of it. And I'm not just remembering and relying on recollections of the kind of mental processes I had at that time. It happened to me at what by my time is only an hour or two ago. I came back into the cave and I saw the sphere was there! I came to it to get into it. And on the way I passed the headless skeleton. I looked at it as I passed it and wished it wasn't there, with all that it implied. I was returning. I was climbing through the cave again across the rocks."

From their expressions as they stood looking at me in the laboratory that they must all but have lived in and occupied almost night and day for fourteen days I saw that they were realizing for the first time that something real had happened to me during the period I had been away.

Real not only for me but for them. Except for the missing skull.

XXV

THE PROJECTION room in the university was blue with smoke. The lights were on, and round the room were tables at which sat the Reckman's staff of Intelligence department's recordists and transcribers. On the screen was a faded picture, disregarded now the lights were on and all but obliterated by the competing midnight illumination. It was a picture they had had to send a camera to get to check my story, the cave with a now headless skeleton, but no one had looked at it for a long time, not since they had lowered the lights temporarily and flashed it on there when it came back from processing in the middle of my telling of the story that it confirmed.

"So I came back from the Outlands," I said. "I had been there, why? On a mission for us? On a mission from Center

City? And I lay under that rock again, waiting for the night to end and looked up into the night sky and felt what I was telling you until that rotating beam flashed out . . ."

"You stayed there the night and then came back to the cave, Major?" the General said. "It's that we're interested in, what you did, and not your feelings."

"Yes, sir!" I said. "It seems to me it was part of it."

"Why?" said Strassen.

They were tense after the time I had taken in the detailed telling of it all. A day had elapsed since I had come back, a day broken by one period of rest and one experiment, but a day without let-up so that everything that happened seemed part of a constant and continuous process. The General was grim-faced and Strassen was sharp and light. I quitted my place by the screen, where I had stood while I told my story. I had finished my narrative if they wanted to take it that way. I went to sit with Galbraith and Sara and Reckman on the chairs. Our company had ceased to be a lecture, a report, and become a conference, though the time was midnight: it was true, as it had been from the beginning, that we did not know how much time we had.

"Why?" said Strassen, insistently.

I looked at him across the semi-circle of the chairs and through the cloud of blue smoke from Galbraith's pipe.

"Because that was part of it, to my mind," I said. "Just who those people I heard as voices were, and what risk they took, and why they took it, when they allowed me to come back to my own time. Because my inference from everything that has happened so far is this: that if we *do* succeed in discovering what we did, our people in our time, to cause the earth to erupt, and its atomic fires to burn more fiercely and send out the radiation that causes a genetic rift, then their world, and that particular future that they belong to, will cease to be."

Galbraith shifted his big head, took his pipe from his mouth and glanced at me. "It's done something to you, Judgen. You're bigger now."

"Voices!" General Bridger's tone crackled. "You're a serviceman, Major. I thought you were a good one. You should know what to think of those!"

"Sir!" I said, "I think that's what worried them: that, without knowing what we were doing, we were playing with the fate of worlds!"

We watched one another. We saw one another as people, not as government departments secretly involved. We were on the edge of human understanding too, and I saw Sara's face slowly set, as though she were coming to a decision. She had been unusually silent while I had told my story and after it, but I waited for her to speak now.

Strassen came in first. He said, "It follows. I told you before we started that if the future exists, so that we can photograph it and even go there, then everything we do, whatever it is, must conspire to produce that future. It is the inevitability, the predetermination of cause and effect, which is the basis of all science. But there is only one way we can break that chain of logic. This future, as we have learned about it, must cease to exist and be supplanted by another."

Sara broke in there. She cut across Strassen:

"I have made up my mind! I am sorry if this disappoints anyone, but I am going to step out of this. I am resigning my connection with the synchrotron! I'm going to find some other work!"

Galbraith looked at her quickly, his dark eyes shooting across to her as they sat beside me.

"That does disappoint me. There was one experiment I wanted to do. Just one more! I hoped we'd work tomorrow."

The General was already speaking harshly over Galbraith's voice.

"You can accuse me of not being squeamish! I can't respect these qualms. Major, I did not expect to have to remind you that your allegiance is to your own time!" I thought he had finished, but he hadn't. His voice rose a shade and took on a note of dedicated passion: "Look at this, all of you! Look around you here! This is real. This is us! I'm not saying that all Judgen experienced is an evil dream, from the time he left here in that sphere to the time that he returned.

138

But it has not a comparable reality! You look at one another and ask yourselves what you're working for in the here and now!"

His hard, sharp eyes fell on me as he said that, then moved across to Sara.

I knew what he meant all right.

Galbraith also looked at me.

"That skeleton has already lost its reality in one particular," he said. "It has lost its head! It is neither here nor there!"

We were talking about Sara. They were telling me clearly what I already knew, that for those bird-named voices to come into existence those events must transpire that included that Sara should become the skeleton.

They were forcing a clear choice on me, on themselves, on all of us.

Only Strassen was thinking ahead now, pursuing a line of his own with his special brand of logic.

"I was thinking of that! There are two conclusions we can come to from the disappearance of the skull. One is that actual and permanent transfer of solid objects from one time to another is just impossible! There are implications here. If we had gotten that skull, and it had proved to be Sara's by any tests we cared to make, we never would have sent it back again! It would have been coexistent in our own time, a skull in life and its counterpart after death, and that is an affront to reason! Why is it? Because those two skulls, the very atoms and material in them, would have gone on, from our time forward; and there would, even in eternity, have been no point of origin for the second one: until the first one, that is now in Sara, live, became a skeleton and lay there, then disappeared, and that would imply that there would positively have to be that future!"

"And the second alternative?" Galbraith said, looking at Strassen curiously, as though he were a brilliant child, not very stable yet, but doing well.

"The alternative!" Strassen said. He looked at Galbraith and then at me. "It is the one alternative that fits the facts.

That skull should never have been sent back! It should have gone on existing as a conditional future, a future that was dependent on a single event that has not yet transpired in time. But it was sent back! Judgen forgot everything else when he first arrived, but he did not forget that! He sent it back. But it did not arrive! And that proves, and only can prove, that that particular future does not exist!"

"Conditionally," I said. "Conditional on our discovering what it was we did to cause their world, and then not doing it. Otherwise, you'd better keep a sharp look-out on the floor of the laboratory. The skull may just arrive!"

XXVI

THE NEXT DAY was the day Sara had her toothache and decided she must see her dentist, and the day I went to Nevada.

He got the plane, commandeered it virtually, using the General's name; I flew it. After we left Tennessee, it was the plain beneath us.

"You're sure you're right?" he said. "Why me?"

"What else?" I said. "You expect me to bring the General? Why didn't you tell him before you used his name to get this plane?"

He looked at me across the cabin of the small army-cooperation aircraft.

"He might have agreed, he might not," he said.

"Exactly," I said. "But worse than that. If I told him what I'm telling you, he might have felt it necessary to go as far as the President to get some action. And by that time, it could have been too late."

"Is that all?"

He was watching me as I flew the machine, keeping the engine-revs just above the point that someone had intended to be the maximum.

"If it's anyone's mistake, it's your department's. I thought I'd give you the chance to rectify it."

"How's that?" He was listening to me carefully, not ready to say yes or no.

"You remember what those people told me, Selwyn and Liebnitz? They gave me some spiel not only about our departmentalism, our segregation and sectarianism in science, which they seemed to infer meant that we don't let our right hand know what our left is doing. They said there was something else. We called the thing Security. It shut off criticism. It meant that projects went forward without being subject to proper scrutiny from the origins of scientific knowledge across the world." I looked at Reckman.

"That isn't true. We take care to bring the experts in. It's only a question of who has clearance."

"Sure. What kind of experts?"

"Enough. All the experts on the lists, in government employment, and on that line." He spoke slowly and deliberately above the engine roar: "The papers are passed to them for just that purpose. For scrutiny and criticism. And more than that. To check the mathematics."

"And the men in other lines?"

"What do you expect us to do? Clear chemical employees in armaments factories for possession of our most recent developments in atomic physics?"

"Something like that. Remember what they said? About their genetic rift and the cause of the radiation from the earth? It would take a paleontologist, a geo-physicist and an atomic scientist working together to see it. But your paleontologist and your geo-physicist wouldn't have clearance. They wouldn't be allowed to know what you were doing with atomic bombs or even that there was a risk."

He was silent. I could see him regretting that he had given way to my urgency and urging and taken the General's plane on what must seem to him a wild-goose chase across the country on something remote from what we were doing.

I told him what I had told him before:

"It's got to be something that will stimulate the underground nuclear forces of the earth."

"I've agreed to investigate it with you," he said. "You can't expect me to believe it."

"What would start up the earth's atomic forces? Suppose you regard the earth as an atomic pile, producing internal heat and powering all volcanoes. There's a molten furnace down there. Not just pockets of uranium scattered in the rocks. We've got past that view in recent years. The drift currents and the electrical and neutron flow in the earth's atomic furnace cause the earth's magnetic field. If you want to stimulate an atomic pile it's a good idea to introduce a source of neutrons, ions."

He watched me flying the plane, which was the job I had been originally trained to do.

"You know a lot about this?"

"Studying the ionic layers and the theory of the earth's magnetic field plays a big part in space flight."

He almost wanted to believe. I could see it. But it was the wrong idea from the wrong source. I did not have a degree from any university in geo-physics and the people who did have the degrees did not have the special knowledge he and I had of what we were doing in terms of ballistic missiles and thermo-nuclear warheads. "You can't get past it," he said. "We have the word of all the experts that these bombs won't produce more than the equivalent of fifty megatons of T.N.T. And that, the geologists tell us, is not even the power of a small volcano."

"All right," I said.

He hung on while the plane dipped in a small air pocket. We could see the mountains up ahead.

"How do you get past it?"

"Your geologists are thinking of these thermo-nuclear devices they explode underground in Nevada as just that, as so many megatons of T.N.T. They are thinking of physical, explosive forces. That's why I said not "geologist" but "geophysicist": a man who will calculate not only physical forces and pressure waves but also the release of hard rays and a flow of penetrative neutrons from dirty bombs."

I checked the altimeter and the fuel gauge. It was awkward. We were going to have to land for gas. I saw he did not answer.

"We know less about our earth," I said; "even a geophysicist knows less about the interior of our earth beyond ten miles down than a cosmologist knows about the interior of a red-dwarf star at a distance of fifty million parses."

I had him coming round. He said: "I do know about this particular batch of bombs they're exploding underground tomorrow in Nevada. The reason they're not exploding them in the atmosphere is that they're particularly dirty bombs."

It lasted while we landed to take on fuel and then he thought again after we had climbed and hung in the sky above the Utah mountains.

"I don't believe you," he said. "I can't believe our men would make a mistake like that."

"It's the kind of mistake they said we would make."

"I don't believe you."

We flew on through the day and it was the same when we saw the Nevada slopes, the area inside a cordon on the surface, of barren empty land where they had had dug deep mine shafts beneath the hills and had a semi-circle of tiny huts facing out towards a mountain slope. On the surface we would never have got inside that cordon. We would have stopped at the first fence, been halted by our lack of special passes. But they did not shoot down the army plane as I circled once and came in to land on their special strip in the middle of all that wild and open country.

The huts looked bigger from the ground. They had messrooms for mining engineers and special bunk-houses for all the scientists who were to observe. Aircraft had been pouring in all that day. We were just another, but I had to make our weight felt. "We are working under the personal orders

143

of General Bridger," I told the Colonel who formed the barrier who should have stopped us. "You can check with Washington. Judgen and Reckman under Bridger from the proton-synchrotron. Something new has come up in our line of atomics there. We have to investigate its specific relation to these bombs."

It was a bluff. It was a bluff that would work so long as they communicated with Washington and not with Bridger. All he knew was that we had gone and taken his personal plane. We had to work fast, and we could not work fast even when I inserted myself in a group of the higher scientists and told them that we had special information derived from our work on the synchrotron that their bombs would leak a penetrative radiation into the earth with unknown results.

They were interested. They gathered around, a group of unoccupied scientists round a table in a staff-hut waiting for the show that was to be put on the following day under the mountain slope across which the shadows had descended across the valley. But they discovered rapidly that I did not know enough and someone came in and said: "Are you the man under General Bridger? A message came through to say he's on his way here." He looked at me significantly and said: "You don't seem to be in good odor with him," And one of the scientists said: "What exactly are these results you've been getting with the synchrotron?" I felt it was all up after that. They were right, of course. I was making charges about their bombs and I had nothing to substantiate them with except a story that I guessed would cause them to put me in a mad-house if I told it. Reckman had gone off and was making some security investigation, which I felt sure was futile and irrelevant, of his own.

General Bridger arrived, and I knew it when I got a call to go at once to the C.O.'s office. He was more grimly sorrowful than angry.

"I had hopes of you, Judgen," he said. "That you were equable, balanced and reliable. This finishes you, I guess. I've come here personally instead of having you arrested to get back my plane. All the way to Nevada at the cost of diverting a special jet, but that's for your past record and not making any allowance for your actions now. What is this hare-brained story you've been telling?"

I told him, and he said: "Why didn't you leave it to the judgment of the men who know? Why didn't you tell it to me, and I'd have had it wired out here for investigation?"

"I thought the investigation would have to be personal and immediate and on the spot," I said. "Sent over the wires it would have the shape of an inquiry best answered by exploding the bombs and telling you what happened tomorrow morning."

He gave me a hard look, grim-faced with experience. "What else do you think will happen now?" he said. "You think even I could order an investigation of the atomics departments and their procedures that wouldn't take months or years? It's a pity Judgen. I liked you. I thought you had the balance and something more, but you've finished yourself now not only for this kind of work but for the rocket strip."

Reckman came in at that point, entering the Nevada testing ground C.O.'s office.

"You!" the General said. "You are the one who ordered my pilot to come to me while you took my plane."

"It's as well I did," Reckman said. "General, can you stop these bomb tests?" He had a file in his hands and he laid it on the table.

General Bridger looked hard at him and Reckman looked back.

"I don't know," Reckman said. "It's only that things are beginning to add up a little. I don't know about these tests. I'm not an expert. It's an interesting story. I have it here." He tapped the file.

"You need more than a story to stop bomb tests that have been laid on at the cost of multi-million dollars," the General said.

"It begins in Siberia eighteen months ago," said Reckman. "An agent of ours. He was nothing very special. We might have wondered about it when he brought off the coup. The complete specification of a new Russian device for increasing the power of thermo-nuclear bombs. Considering he'd never been particularly bright before my department might have wondered, I know I would myself, how he got such a thing so easily. What would you do, General, if one of our inventors came up with a device so new, so basic and so simple, that it would be too dangerous to test it in any test you could observe?"

The General stared at him. For an instant he was rigid, then his eyes took on a haunted look.

"Not leak it to the Russians!" he said. But it was an answer he gave in hope, still thinking.

"No?" Reckman sat down before the file. "It would have advant ;es, General," he said insidiously. "You would be able to use the device if the other side tested it and survived. You'd shed no tears if they tested it and didn't. And it isn't you, you see, it's them. They know we can destroy them anyway. What have they got to lose, by showing us that they can do the same? A dilemma for us? Our doubt about whether their device works or not? They may not know—but we have to know!" He tapped the file. "It's here, General. This is the file on these tests. This is what they are all about."

I watched General Bridger. It was new to him. I could see it by his haunted look. And yet what could he do? Even if we were right, the situation was still the same. The Russians had no need to try the device until it came to warfare, but since they had it, we most certainly had. And yet if we were right . . . I watched him. It was he now who was suffering the temptation I had felt, the choice between the good of his country and the good of humanity at large.

Yet I saw it. I had an awful sense of it. Because of what he was, it was inevitable what he had to say.

"The tests must go on. Reckman, that is final!"

Despair, I thought? But there was something more. He looked straight at both of us. "You will go back to Tennessee," he said. "You will take the jet. These are your orders. Galbraith has thought of something, some new crucial experiment at noon tomorrow. You will observe"

"An experiment!" I said.

He looked at me.

He turned to Reckman. "You will observe there," he said, "while I watch this end."

He was putting the two things together, I saw. Even he! He was connecting them despite himself.

But what he said dryly to Reckman was: "If there are any developments here, I'll let you know!" It was despair. Or a haunted feeling that he should do something. Yet all he did about it was to stay in Nevada while he sent us back to Tennessee.

As though, I thought, that were useful now!

XXVII

I CANNOT HOPE to describe, to do justice to those final scenes in the laboratory.

Sara, sitting at the control desk, looked across to me and nodded. It was an answer to my silent question about what had happened at the dentist the previous day.

I was incredulous. I could not believe they were doing it. I had a sense of fatality, of inevitability, of finality. But that, I learned in the underground laboratory, where we had only arrived as it was beginning, was what it was all about.

We had only just arrived after travelling through the night and morning, and yet it was as though we had never been away. Galbraith came forward.

"In Nevada!" I said. I wondered if anyone would understand. I looked even at Sara accusingly.

He stopped me interrupting her, even then, in the midst of the work she was already doing, while he told me: "Don't blame Sara, Judgen. I have asked her, told her she must complete this series of experiments. She can't refuse!"

"But now!" I said. I turned to Strassen as he worked at the barrier wall in the familiar surroundings of the laboratory with its machines and mirrors. Someone, I thought, must have retained some sanity. I looked at Sara again and she shook her head at me. Galbraith was right. When he asked a final piece of work from her she could not refuse him. I went to Strassen.

"What are you doing?" I said. "Are you determined to help it—to prove that events are predestined? Even faced with a material future, do you have to give it a material cause?" I could think of nothing else.

He turned to me from the mirror and his controls.

"There is no choice!" he said. He looked at me sardonically. "We're driven by our own causes, Judgen—haven't you realized that yet? We're as predictable as the motions of the stars—as the behavior of a rabbit when it's driven by the chemistry of its glands. It's what I told you: that every moment of the future is determined by the causes in the past!" But then he looked at Galbraith. "Except that he doesn't believe me," he told me. "Even that works out. Because he doesn't believe me, he says he's going to prove it—and so he fulfills it!"

Standing in the laboratory with Reckman, I turned to Galbraith. I realized it then. He was the clue. He held the answer. His was the major part. I saw it now.

"You are doing this to prove Strassen wrong?" I said. I looked at Sara and the control desk. "You think you've found a way?"

In his laboratory he looked at me calmly and formidably. It was he I had to talk to, to understand.

"It's an experiment of classical simplicity. I'm surprised we didn't think of it before," he calmly told me.

What I thought of was of the General in Nevada, and of the situation in the laboratory, so like the cave. I was sure of it now. I could not let it happen. I had to hold him up.

Except that they went on setting up the experiment as we talked.

"To prove or disprove an academic theory, Professor— even a metaphysical theory—you risk all this!"

"An academic point?" He answered me while Sara and Strassen went on working, talking while a deep hum began to fill the laboratory from the great magnetic core.

"You call it an academic point, whether man has free will or not, whether we can control the future or whether we are in its control?" he said. His eyes looked keenly at me.

"But that is it!" I said. "Perhaps that is just it, that we only *think* we have free will!"

"Why?" he said. He looked hard at me, compelling my attention. "Because a biochemist tells you that life itself is only an extension of atomic matter? Because a behaviorist says your behavior is a conditioned reflex? Have you been listening to Strassen? Do you truly think you're quite predictable, Judgen, because you're the son of your fathers and wear their kind of clothes and think their thoughts?"

He was talking in abstractions yet Sara was working at the control panel then and there.

"Does that matter, Professor. This is it! Does that truly matter? Compared to this?" I waved a hand.

He was a man of power. I had seen it. I had seen him deal with other people. And now, as he looked at me grimly, he dealt with me. It was not only what he said:

"It matters," he told me. "Listen! If Strassen is right and the future is predestinate and predictable, then the universe is what he says it is. Not merely material, but mechanical! Do you like that, Judgen? To be part of a piece of clockwork that is running down? But suppose it isn't! Suppose a man, by his will and choice, can alter the future in any little way? Then the converse holds. Do you think we do this for nothing? Is it nothing if a man can act by will alone, produce material events with no material cause? Are you a

149

fool, Judgen, or can you not see that the whole universe is contained in that? It is the transcendental question. For if one event can happen in the universe that has *no* material cause, then there is something more than matter and material!"

"But what?" He had caught me. I was struggling in my mind. I saw Sara looking at me for a moment with sympathy. In this apparently we were together.

"Are you trying to produce a scientific proof of God, Professor? A life-force? A spirit or something beyond the laws of solid matter!" I was awed.

He looked at me strangely. "If we could do that," he said. "Wouldn't it be something greater than any risk?" And then he turned. He knew he had me. He turned to Strassen: "Go?" It was it, the time.

Strassen was working his machinery to establish a camera on the plinth. It was another of those experiments. To me it seemed just another. And yet . . . The camera was in the old bell-jar. I could see it in the mirrors, turned back on us.

"Ready," said Strassen, calm in the laboratory. "Ready now to go."

The camera, I saw, looking in the mirrors, was turned to give a view of the clock on the laboratory wall above us, and of all our actions. And Sara was now totally engaged at her control desk. Galbraith looked at her with an expression of intentness and concentration.

"Ready, Sara?"

"Go," said Sara, watching only what she was doing now. Yet she glanced at me.

"Go!"

The laboratory clock said noon. I saw Sara's hand go down and I sensed a deeper note in the hum that filled the laboratory and all the underground chambers of the synchrotron. I looked quickly through the mirrors at the camera in the bell-jar, then back at the clock.

The clock hand moved to a little beyond the hour. After an elapse of one minute nothing was visible around the camera and the bell-jar, but after that I began to see it, the formation of the silver mist again, the enclosing sphere that in a matter of minutes would remove camera and bell-jar from our sight.

"What is this experiment?" I said. "What are you doing this time?" But no one answered me.

It was three minutes after the hour now, and the mist around the camera and bell-jar, as seen through the mirrors, was preceptible now. But Galbraith began to act. He performed a simple action that seemed to me inexplicable. He stood for a while in thought, as though deciding just what to do, and then he walked across our side of the laboratory, took a chair and placed it against the wall, and climbed upon it.

Reaching up to the clock, he stopped it. While the fingers were registering a little beyond three minutes after the hour, he stopped them, then moved them back to noon and held them until the clock stopped, and then got down.

He looked at his watch.

"Keep the experiment going one more minute," he said, "then ease everything down. We want to get the camera back and get the film out and examine it right away."

It was a little, simple thing, so easy when you knew.

XXVIII

I HAD A ghastly sense of the ticking seconds.

They were using a viewer in the laboratory.

We were crowded together, in the small space and angle from which it was possible to watch the viewer screen.

It was showing the experiment we had just seen, but from the camera angle, looking back at us. The laboratory was visible in a diminished picture on the screen, with all of us present in it in the places we had occupied, and the clock above us on the wall.

The clock was tiny in the picture, but just large enough for us to see the time clearly by it. I wondered why.

"The significance of this experiment," Galbriath said, "is that at this time, as you see it now, with the experiment beginning, I had not decided what I was going to do. That is the essence. That is why I could not tell you in advance."

He watched. The experiment as seen in the viewer had begun now. The clock hands had begun to move forward past noon and there was a visible speeding up of their movement and of our actions in the picture, as always when seen from the position of the forming sphere.

"I thought I would stand with a handkerchief held above my head," Galbraith said. There was a strange dry tension and excitement in his voice. "But at this point, now, I decided I would stop the clock!"

His movements were fast in the picture we were watching. He moved all right, but it was not possible to see what he did. He had become a blur. The clock was not a blur, however. It was clear with its fingers marking three minutes after the hour, and moving on.

Then I looked and looked again. I could not believe what I was seeing.

For the clock hands, seen clearly in the diminished picture on the screen, were sweeping on inexorably. They were moving faster as they always did, or had. But this time I knew that the clock had been stopped.

The future, I thought? It had been the future at the time it was recording it. It was something else now.

Who had said . . . ? It was Reckman, when we had first seen the pictures, talking to the General in the car. "What the Professor has been showing us is impossible." But he had not seen anything then!

I could not understand it. The camera showed us a future that had been going to happen—and yet one that had not in fact happened.

In that incredible situation, it was Strassen's ideas about

the universe that were most affronted. He swept round on Galbraith.

"You knew!" It was amazement, incredulity, more than wonder. "You knew—you even guessed that something like this would happen?"

Galbraith looked at him first, quietly. It was truth, not triumph: "Yes, this is it, isn't it?" he quietly said. "The future you thought was fixed and final! By will and effort it can be changed."

I felt dazed and dazzled, trying to understand.

"The future?" I said. I fought for words. "You call it the future—but what do you mean by that?"

At least I could accept it, though Strassen could not.

"But what?" he said, astounded. He was deeply shaken. He looked not like a man who had been conducting a scientific experiment, but like a man who had seen a ghost. "You mean that is the nature of the future?"

He made a tremendous attempt to pull himself together:

"Yet it was some kind of forecast! What else could it be? It showed a future—but a future with the clock going!"

He looked unbelievingly at the viewer, where the short film had run out and coiled itself around its spool.

"Listen," Galbraith said. He quietly looked at all of us. "It showed the future as it was at the beginning of the experiment." He paused. "Not the future as it was in the middle of the experiment, when I took a hand and altered it. Think! That is the nature of the future!"

I looked at him dazedly. The others were doing the same. We saw it was.

And then I realized: or thought I did, suddenly.

"You mean the cave—and Center City, and the Outlands—that's what the Voices were afraid of—it could be changed?" I had a tremendous vision.

He looked at me closely and severely, not agreeing.

"So easily, Judgen? You think we could change all that so easily? How much thought do you think it took on my part to invent this experiment, to stop the clock? Don't you realize what this means? The future is built up gradually from the past! A whole world you saw, not just a clock! A million inevitabilities. And I changed the future in one tiny way!"

I tried to understand it. A world, I thought. A future that was built up, little by little, from the past. A future, he meant, that came into being slowly! Already the future existed, even a hundred years from now. We made it. We drew it like an artist drew a picture . . . Yet what he seemed to say was that we could change it, like an artist who scraped off his oils and repainted a little detail . . . But that still left my world, my world of Center City, which I had thought the experiment disposed of, still intact! I looked around for Reckman, to ask him what he had said exactly to the General and myself on that first day when we were sitting in the car.

Reckman was not there! I looked around, but he seemed to have gone out. And Galbraith was talking.

It was not to any one of us. It might have been to himself.

"A future that is predictable and inevitable," he was saying. "A great canvas already painted in its outlines. It is, in all its great events. The tides. The majestic movements of the stars. The shape of the Galaxy, that can be predicted for a million years. But life, the little and new thing . . . Some spirit? Or God in the shape of an uncertainty principle that is growing. The rest of the universe runs down from hot to cold, but life builds up. Greater . . . We can shape the small events and may someday shape the big ones. And yet our future hangs upon us. It hangs upon you, Sara, like a heavy imminence. I thought to remove it by this experiment, and now I see I did not . . ."

Reckman came back then. He had been called out to receive a message.

XXIX

THE ULTIMATE. The mercy.

It was hard to believe it when it happened.

Reckman re-entered the laboratory. He hardly looked at anyone. He came to me. "For you!" he said.

He handed me a message, with a world of meaning.

I looked at his face, at the others who stood around. I opened the message and slowly read it.

It was the news from Nevada:

"BOMB TESTS TO CONTINUE AS ORDERED. BUT NOT NEVADA. CHANGE. NOW INTENDED OUT OF ATMOSPHERE. IN SPACE. SUGGESTED OVER RUSSIA.

BRIDGER

I looked at the paper in my hand.

I seemed to see General Bridger, haunted after a sleepless night, deciding . . .

The words seemed to blaze on the paper. I felt sick, it looked like such relief. I wondered only if it was enough. "Over Russia . . ." It did not seem the end.

I looked around the laboratory. We were still there. I believed it had done that. It was the reason we were still alive.

I turned to Galbraith with the signal.

"He says *a change*," I said. "But is it? Is this something too that will only change the future in a small way?" I asked as though he could know.

He read the signal and passed it on to Sara.

Reckman spoke with quiet intensity: "That's what the

General wants to know! I heard him on the phone. But he wants more than Judgen. He wants to know if this has changed the pictures you get with the synchrotron, or if this too is wasted effort!"

We all looked at Reckman.

And then we saw it, how the General too had thought, had wondered, even trying it at last to see if the kind of action he could take made any change.

"All right!" said Galbraith. "Francis! Strassen!"

He had the determination to try again.

And the experiment was almost set up. With everything there, we had it ready. I saw Sara dare to smile. Her eyes were full of longing. She showed eagerness and hope. At last maybe the clouds were falling away from round her. There was a chance now, I could see she believed. A chance of changing fate . . .

"Do you still think we can't do anything against predictions?" I asked her in those moments as she went back to her control desk. "Do you know?" her eyes asked.

"A delayed run with the self-processing camera?" Strassen was saying to Galbraith. They were fixing the technical details: "A still would do!"

"Run up!" said Galbraith to Sara as she reached her desk. I watched her hands cross the control board.

I had bitter qualms. I thought what the experiment would mean if the camera came back and showed us the scene in the cave as it was before, just as I had left it. What would we do then? Get Sara out, I thought! This was the last. I was determined to stop it now. The future—I clung to the thought—could be changed in small ways.

Big ones? We did not know.

The magnetic hum deepened again. I thought of my Voices in the Outlands, of Teal and Widgeon. They had not wanted Widgeon to let me come back in time. They knew, I realized, what we were only finding out. But Widgeon had sent me back. He believed that I could only change his time in small ways, if at all . . .

The sphere around the camera darkened as we watched it

156

in the mirrors. The camera and its container vanished, and then came back.

Came back? We could not believe it.

We looked with horror at the fading sphere, straining unbelieving to see the plinth. It seemed disaster.

The bell-jar had been smashed as though crushed by an iron hand, and the camera too!

We strained to see, not even understanding yet what we were seeing.

Strassen cried out. We looked at what had come back to us with nameless horror.

Strassen had the best view through the mirrors above the wall. He had seen first and, despite himself, he understood it. "The cave isn't there any more!" he declared to us. "The camera—the bell-jar! It looks as though we've tried to smash them through a hillside, to insert them bodily into solid rock!"

He turned and looked at Galbraith, and so did we all But Galbraith was simply looking through the mirrors at the wreck.

"The future has changed," he said. "We have no access now to . . . to the situation in the cave. It's gone!"

We knew that. It came to all of us, quickly or slowly. The coincidence of this following the General's signal was too much. The cause and effect in it was apparent even to Strassen, even though he tried to refuse to believe it.

Sara spoke. She had stood by Galbraith loyally, even at the end. Now the cave had gone, and she was still there, she might have been permitted a reaction. But she said:

"The future's changed, but changed to what?"

"How much has it changed?" Reckman said. He took up the point. "The General's going to want to know, Professor! Has it changed in detail, or is there going to be quite another future?"

Galbraith simply looked at him. It was as apparent to Reckman as to anyone what had happened when he had tried to find out. If the future of the place where the synchrotron was situated was to be solid rock, than that was all they were likely to find out now with Galbraith's machine, unless they built another.

"If we build another synchrotron," Galbraith said quietly, "it still may lead to solid rock, or out to some point in space. We don't know! We are still ignorant entirely of the kind of warp this machine sets up in time."

Reckman looked dazed at the prospect of building another synchrotron, at a cost of hundreds of millions, at a site chosen at random, and with unknown results. But that was again the way it was about the future.

Sara had come to me. I took her hand in mine. It was coming to us that we had reached an impasse. She had not left her work, but found it ended suddenly.

We could go! I could hardly believe it but that was the way it was. We could go with the world still there and the future now unknown!

Even so, I spoke: suddenly very desperate.

"Professor, that world was very real!"

Galbraith looked at me suddenly, somberly. He should have been glad, I thought. We were relieved, after all, of the threat of the situation in the cave.

"So is the arms race!" Galbraith grimly said to me.

He did not say any more, and yet I understood. What had he told me? That the future was built up, little by little, from the past. I thought again of Widgeon and Teal and my bird-named voices. They would not have allowed me to come back if they had thought that the future, my future and their present, could be changed in its entirety.

The cave was gone. But the world of Center City and the Outlands might still be there, an inevitable product not of one but of many causes! It might or it might not. We could not know! It could be that the General's signal indicated a change in human history. But they were still going to hold the bomb tests, he said, in space, over Russia; and then, inevitably, if the world went on as it was, there would be others.

I realized what Galbraith meant. We had not *proved anything* about the future. We were back where we started. And it was only that we did not know. Yet the world of Center City would be hanging over us always now.

Perhaps it too was a threat that always had been there!

I turned, and put my arm round Sara's waist. She looked up at me. "It's as well I have you, Howard!" she said. "It looks as though I'm out of a job! This synchrotron is finished. But I can't say I'm sorry!"

She moved as I took her out.

We came out, out of the underground passages. We emerged to the view of Lake Valley, the sunlight, and the open air.

"It's time!" she said. "I told you I was giving up!"

It was not what she meant exactly. But I understood as we looked out on the world together.

* * *

For that is the way it is today.

Sara and I are living at the rocket base now. In April we expect what we hope will be the first of our many, and, we fervently hope, quite normal children. In May there is just a chance that I may become the second or third man to make a circuit of the moon. The General has come round to me again, following his decision about Nevada. And although they are building another synchrotron on the pattern of Lake Valley, on a more open but at the same time less exposed site, it will not be finished for about three years, so in the meantime his guess about the future, or yours, is just as good as mine.

And meanwhile there is only one other thing.

They hope to know more about the interior of the earth, and just how it could be affected by the explosion of nuclear bombs below the surface, when they have completed the Mohole boring, but they aren't waiting for it of course.

You may have heard of it. As an off-shore boring, down

through the sea-bed where the crust of the earth is thin, it is a project expected to add greatly to our knowledge of the earth's interior.

If the Senator gets the appropriation, that is. Otherwise the people I talk to seem happy to go on knowing nothing. They prefer quite blindly to take the risk.